BUS STOP BABY

Also by Fleur Hitchcock

The *Shrunk!* Adventures
Shrunk!
Shrunk! Mayhem & Meteorites
Shrunk! Ghosts on Board
Sunk!

and

The Trouble with Mummies
The Yoghurt Plot

BUS STOP BABY

FLEUR HITCHCOCK

Piccadilly
PRESS

First published in Great Britain in 2016 by
PICCADILLY PRESS
80-81 Wimpole St, London W1G 9RE
www.piccadillypress.co.uk

A CIP catalogue record for this book is
available from the British Library.

ISBN: 978-1-4714-0350-7
also available as an ebook

1 3 5 7 9 10 8 6 4 2

Typeset in Sabon by Palimpsest Book Production Limited, Falkirk,
Stirlingshire

Printed and bound by Clays Ltd, St Ives Plc

Piccadilly Press is an imprint of Bonnier Publishing Fiction,
a Bonnier Publishing company
www.bonnierpublishingfiction.co.uk
www.bonnierpublishing.co.uk

For Jane and Ellen, whose story is not the same

Author Note

Foundlings have always fascinated me. I think, as a small child, I confused them with changelings, and thought that they had something to do with the fairies. They are all children who arrive on doorsteps, from nowhere. Often found at night, often only found by the sound of their cry. It seemed romantic.

I started to collect their stories.

A man I met claimed to have been found on the doorstep of the village policeman on Christmas day. The policeman and his wife went on to bring him up.

The story of a baby found in a phone box – again, at Christmas.

A child left in the crib of a church.

And then I came across all the tales of children from the Foundling Museum. Stories of people who sought birth mothers, and made lives with adoptive families. Many hundreds of them, lost and found.

But I'd always wondered what it would be like to find a foundling. Would you, in some way, become a part of that child's life? Would you, just for a moment, become a kind of parent?

And so Amy came along.

The cloth was only a dishcloth and the girl was only young as she dabbed gently at the little creature on the straw bale. She rinsed the cloth in the pail of warm water. Water she'd tested with her elbow like she knew she should, even though she had no idea what it ought to feel like.

'There now,' she said, washing away the blood and the strange white stuff that no one had ever mentioned.

'There now.'

She laid the baby on a towel, it squealed but it didn't scream, and she wondered when it would be hungry.

It should last a little while before they had to try feeding it.

She plunged her hands into the bucket; a piece of straw floated free and water splashed over the sides, wetting the baby, wetting the towel. She decided that her attempts at washing were enough, although there was still a stubborn patch on the baby's head. An apple-shaped patch that perhaps was a birthmark, or perhaps a mark of birth. Whatever, she couldn't shift it. She rubbed the damp from the baby's skin, picked the baby up, wrapped it another towel and kissed it.

'Good luck little girl,' she said as brightly as she could. 'Good luck.'

Chapter 1

The minibus drops us at the edge of the village.

Eden gets off first and I follow, my feet crunching frozen grass at the side of the road.

'Night, girls,' says the driver, closing the door behind us. He checks his mirror and the minibus pulls away down the lane into the darkness. The red tail-lights bounce along the lane, wink in and out of hedgerows and then vanish.

Above me, the sky is indigo. Clean, with a slim crescent moon hanging between the telephone wires. A crow flies across the moon, heading for a distant group of trees. Stillness creeps over the landscape and I stay, letting the cold sink in, watching the dark, listening to the quiet. My back turned towards the village and its points of light.

After all, I'm in no hurry to get home.

I hear Eden cross the road behind me and someone in the village opening and closing a door.

A cat squeals.

There's a whiff of woodsmoke and I wonder if Dad's already lit our fire. I imagine him glancing at the clock, stopping work, putting on the kettle, and I think for the millionth time about today at school and how he's going to react when I tell him that my brand-new purse has gone. Not only the purse but the brand-new money inside it.

'Amy? Come on,' says Eden from the other side of the road. She pulls her blazer lapels over her chest. 'Don't hang about, it's freezing.'

'I know,' I say. 'I was just —'

'You're going to have to tell him sometime,' she says. She turns her back on me and stomps up the lane towards home. Beyond her, a street lamp flicks on, casting thick yellow light over the lane. It actually makes the village seem colder.

Taking a last look at the little moon hanging in the telephone lines I follow Eden, my bag heavy, my shoes uncomfortable. She's right. I am going to have to tell him. Sooner or later.

The walls along the lane radiate intense cold. The stone is already damp with ice. Kicking at the kerb I wander off the lane, uphill, into the village square. Once again I try to remember all the people near me in the changing room. But I keep coming back to the same person. The only one with a chance to slip their hand in my bag. The only one with a reason.

Isobel.

My friend. My best friend.

Eden's heels ring on the pavement, echoing from the houses, and something else – probably that cat again – mews above us.

Eden stops and turns. Waits for me.

A car slips out of the little street called The Shambles, halfway up the square, and heads down towards the lane we've just walked up from. The driver doesn't switch the headlights on until they're nearly at the bottom of the hill, and the narrow lane seems to catch them by surprise because they brake suddenly, their rear lights washing the church crimson.

I watch the car until it disappears. But I'm not thinking about it. I'm thinking about PE and purses and best friends.

'It's going to kill Dad,' I say.

'It is,' replies Eden. 'He'll be really disappointed.'

'Thanks for your support,' I say.

'Pleasure,' she says.

A huge tractor turns off the main road and grinds past us up the hill. The roar of the engine bounces around the square, so loud we can't hear our footsteps.

We stomp faster, keeping pace, past the church on our left, the empty shop, the concrete bus shelter and the village hall on our right until the tractor driver finally passes us and accelerates away towards The Tyning.

On the crest of the hill, the pub lights up, its *Green Man* sign only just greener than the sky above it. We walk slowly towards it, our breathing the loudest sound except . . .

'Can you hear that cat?' I say. 'Or is it a seagull?'

Eden half turns, listening. 'Seagull. Sounds like it's trapped.'

We wait, our eyes and ears scanning the village. The noise is coming from behind us. 'But we haven't walked past it,' I say. 'I would have noticed.'

'It's probably in somebody's house.'

'I'm going to see,' I say.

'I'll go home without you,' warns Eden. But she stays put at the top of the hill.

Dumping my bag, I walk slowly back down the square towards the village hall. The windows are dark. I stop outside, listening to the village. A cow lows in the distance. A crow calls from the church tower. I listen for the little cry and it comes again, but from somewhere really close. I look up at the windows of the houses, but they all look closed up, cosy, with curtains drawn.

'Waaaaaaaaaa.' The sound is clear but faint. Less like a cat or a gull, more like a lamb. And it's coming from somewhere in the square.

'It's right here,' I say.

'C'mon, Amy – I need a wee. I really want to go home,' Eden calls from the top of the hill.

'Go, then,' I say, listening for the cry again. It seems to be at ground level. To my left.

'Waaa.'

The bus shelter. It has to be the bus shelter.

Standing by the small building, I peer in through one of the glassless windows. It's dark in there although a stretched rectangle of street light reaches across the floor towards the bench at the back. It catches on the names scratched in the brown paint and it catches on a battered cardboard box lying on the stone floor.

I walk around to stand in the entrance. Half of the box is now in my shadow, and I notice the ghost smells that hang around the bus stop. Ice-cold wee and cigarettes.

Eden's heels clatter on the paving behind me. 'What is it?' she pants.

'Only that box.'

We both stare at the box. It's trembling. Just a little.

'What's in it?'

'I don't know,' I say. 'A puppy or something?'

'Open it.'

I hesitate.

'Go on, I doubt it'll bite,' she says, her breath hot on the back of my neck. I reach forward and pull back the flap, expecting a little fluffy thing to leap out.

But it doesn't.

We crane to look inside. Something small and pale flails at the light.

A tiny hand.

'Oh God,' says Eden, standing back. 'It's a baby. Amy, you've found a baby.'

Chapter 2

'Don't touch!' says Eden. 'We should call an ambulance or someone.'

'We can't leave it here. It's freezing,' I say.

'But its mum might come back to look for it,' she says.

'It's not a bird,' I say. 'We can touch it.'

'We should just tell someone. No! Amy!' she yelps as I decide to ignore her, and reach into the box.

'Amy!'

'It'll die, it's been abandoned. We have to . . . Oh!' My fingers close around the baby, grasping the cold limbs inside some sort of covering. I lift it effortlessly; it weighs nothing and I can feel fragile bones beneath the flesh. It seems frozen so I clutch it to my chest for warmth and its fingers immediately grasp my hair. One tiny hand pulling, the other icy against my blouse.

'It's so small,' says Eden behind me.

'Oh – you poor little fruzzed thing,' I say, holding it even closer, trying to fold it into my skin.

'Here – have my jacket.' Eden yanks off her blazer and wraps it around the baby's back, tucking it in all around. 'And my scarf.' She bungs it over the top of the baby's head and grabs my scarf to fill in the gaps.

The baby wails. A weeny cry that I realise I'd been mistaking for a cat. 'I think it's hungry.' I start walking back up the hill towards home.

'We should ring Dad,' says Eden, stopping to get our school bags, groaning as she hitches them both onto her back and struggling along behind me.

'We should just get home,' I say.

'We should stop in the pub . . .' But I don't hear the rest, because the baby sets up a proper wail.

'Oh, baby, don't cry, you're safe now,' I say, pulling back the jacket and peering in. Its tiny creased features look alien under the sodium light and I wonder just how old it is. I know that new babies are all crunkled, and older ones are smoothed out, because Auntie May had a baby last year, and the baby filled up from one visit to the next. This baby is creased and has its eyes closed, and although it's crying it doesn't seem to have tears. I put my little finger against its cheek and it stops squalling. 'Oh, little sweetie,' I say. 'Sorry it's only a finger. But I bet Dad'll know what to feed you.'

We pass the Green Man on our right and I keep

walking as fast as I can. I could run, but I don't dare with the baby in my arms.

Eden pants up next to me. 'Amy – we could go in and call the police.'

'No – it's not open yet – they won't answer the door. '

Eden lets out a sigh of resignation and we scuttle in silence along the lumpy pavements until we see our cottage at the end of Summer Lane, orange squares marking the windows, Dad's shadow upstairs in the workshop.

'I'll go tell him,' says Eden, dropping our bags and running ahead, throwing the front door open so that it crashes into the stairs behind. 'Dad! Dad! Amy's found a baby.'

I hear his feet on the stairs then his voice. 'What?'

'A baby in the bus shelter,' she shouts. 'Look – she's coming with it.'

Dad's silhouette appears in the doorway. 'Amy?' he calls. 'Is this true?'

I stumble up the path, and hold the bundle towards him. He reaches out and touches it but he doesn't take it from me. I can't see his face, but his voice is full of wonder when he speaks. 'A baby.' He stops for a moment – staring at the bundle in my arms. 'A baby?'

He says the words over and over, and then as if he finally registers what it means, Dad springs into life. 'Hold it against you, keep it warm,' he says. He flings open the door to the kitchen, the warmest room of the house. 'Quick, quick, in you go.'

Blinking, I stumble out of the darkness into the warm light.

'It's too cold and too bright for babies in here – hang on,' Dad grabs something from a cupboard and almost instantly the room smells of burned dust. A fan heater I've never seen before whirrs into action in the corner. The overhead lights go off and a single Anglepoise illuminates the table. A pile of towels materialise on the Rayburn, and Dad rushes around boiling kettles and retrieving bags of cotton wool from upstairs.

I stand by the Rayburn, holding the baby, gazing into its folded face. The eyes are closed, and there seems to be a crazy amount of extra skin around them. It looks incredibly old rather than incredibly young. Tiny peely flakes cover its forehead and nose, and peeking out from Eden's jacket are a few spare black hairs.

Eden comes to stand beside me. 'Isn't it amazing?'

'Yes,' I say.

20

'In a squally kind of a way,' she says. 'It's beautiful – so . . . new.'

Dad rings the police from the hall. I hear him talking to them, explaining about the baby, about us.

I hold the baby closer to my chest, it flexes itself against me, seeking warmth.

'It smells of wee,' says Eden. 'Dad? Should we do something about that?'

Dad appears on my other side with a blanket and a towel, which he lays out on the table in a scrumply nest. 'Let's change the poor thing's nappy. Pop it down there on the blankets,' he says. 'Careful with the head, it might be very wobbly, depends how newborn it is.'

I rest the baby in the blanket, Eden's blazer falls away and we all unwrap the scarves. Underneath the baby's wearing a grubby pink Babygro, and Eden's right. It does smell of wee. We stand in a ring not quite daring to touch. 'That's all it had?' says Dad. 'I'm surprised it's still alive.' Unheld, the baby's shoulders hunch and it pulls its elbows and knees in. It's the most vulnerable thing I've ever seen. Weaker than a butterfly or a fledgling. It's so unprotected. So small.

'It was in the bus shelter?' says Dad.

'In a cardboard box,' says Eden.

'God,' says Dad, gently unpopping the Babygro.

21

'How . . . ?' but he's speechless. On the brink of tears. He peels back the dirty pink suit, slipping the arms out and then teasing it away from the baby's feet. Underneath, the baby is purple. Lots of different shades of purple, but purple all the same. In the middle, its tummy button is an ugly black scab. Below that, a teeny-tiny nappy.

'Oooh – is that normal?' says Eden, pointing at the mess around the umbilical cord.

'I can't remember.' Dad cups his warm hands on either side of one of the baby's feet. 'I think there's usually a clip.'

I grab the other foot, blowing on it. 'Icy,' I say.

'Eden – bottom drawer – a clean tea towel, or there might even be one of those muslin squares? We can use that as a nappy. Amy, can you get a towel off the Rayburn and beat it about 'til it's nice and soft? We'll change this little creature and then wrap it up as warmly as we can.' Eden rootles about in a drawer, and I grab a warm blue towel, scumbling it up until the little loops soften. She finds a square of thin white fabric. 'This?' she says.

'Yup.' Dad pings open the fastenings, lifting the baby gently by its ankles. All the time that he does it, he talks softly. Telling it what he's doing, calming and smiling, his voice warm and soft, and the baby opens its eyes. They're dark, possibly blue, with amazing clear whites surrounding them. Dad whisks off the nappy, which is full of dark green spinachy stuff.

'Poo,' he says and mops it off the baby with cotton wool dipped in warm water.

'A girl,' I say. I put my finger out and the baby grabs it, pulling it towards her mouth.

Dad nods. 'A girl.' I glance up at him. He's lost the battle with the tears. A single drop traces down his cheek, falling onto the baby's splotchy skin.

She reaches out, her hand dabbing the air before catching at Dad's finger. He holds her hand and gently kisses it before wrapping her quickly in the homemade nappy and swaddling her in warm towels.

Eden and I watch in silence.

'Do you want to hold her, Amy?' says Dad.

'Can I?' says Eden.

'Of course,' says Dad, wiping the corner of his eye on his cuff. And I realise that we're all being really polite to each other. As if the baby was a special visitor, as if she was royalty. Eden sits in the big chair at the end of the table and holds the baby, rocking her gently. Dad kneels beside her, looking into the baby's slightly open blackbird eyes that gaze up at Eden's chin.

'Can we feed her?' asks Eden.

'I don't have anything to feed her with.'

Before I even know the thought's in my head I say: 'Can we keep her?'

Eden looks over to Dad. 'Can we?' she says. 'Can we adopt her?'

Dad ignores us, crossing to the window just as I hear the roar of a motorbike. 'They're here,' he says, going round to the front door.

A draught of freezing air rushes into the house.

A tall man in green with a motorbike helmet comes into the house. The paramedic.

'A baby, they said?' He takes off his bike helmet and gloves and stares at the baby in Eden's arms.

He too is silenced. Unaware of the audience the baby yawns and lets out a soft cry.

'Girl or boy?' asks the paramedic.

'Girl,' Dad replies.

'Where was she? May I see her?' he reaches for the baby and Eden stands to hand her over.

'We found her in the bus shelter,' I say.

'In a cardboard box,' says Eden. 'A crisp box.'

'Poor little thing,' says the paramedic, cradling the baby and stroking her cheek with his thumb. 'Poor little darling.'

Chapter 3

When he finally arrives, fresh from a burglary, Sergeant Harding takes the briefest look at the baby and sits down at the table to stare at the plastic bag holding a sad pink Babygro. 'Second hand,' he states with great certainty. 'Lucky for her you were dilly-dallying on your way home.'

I nod, but don't look up. They've given her back to me. The paramedic had all the gear, a proper nappy, food, and a Babygro, but they need a baby seat to transport her to hospital so for now it's like the Nativity in our kitchen, except that we're a bit short on sheep and actual mothers.

Eden and I don't really have one.

And the baby definitely doesn't seem to have one.

The baby's eyes are closed; a little bubble of milk goes in and out on her delicate lip with every breath. She must weigh more now because there's a whole bottle of special paramedic milk inside her, but she's still lighter than Eden's guinea pigs. The sounds of the kitchen fade as I watch her face, every twitch, every yawn. Apart from the alarming little heartbeat visible through the skin on the top of her head, everything about her is perfect.

The paramedic's outside, trying to get a phone signal, and the policeman is inside asking us questions, but I let Eden answer. She knows everything. She always does. The baby burps in my arms and a bubble of air passes right through her. I glance up at Dad.

'It's normal,' he says, smiling. 'She's a little gasworks at this stage.'

Slapping his hands against his thighs to warm up, the paramedic comes back in. He, the policeman and Dad talk about the temperature outside. 'So what'll happen to her?' I ask, cutting through the conversation.

'She'll be fostered. Isn't that right?' the paramedic asks the policeman, but they both look vague.

'Oh,' I say, glancing up at Dad, who is making a second pot of tea. 'Can anyone be a foster parent?' I say, but they've moved on to guessing the baby's age.

I rest my finger by the baby's mouth and she twists her lips to touch it.

'Is she still hungry?' asks the paramedic, leaning over us. 'Amazing, isn't she?'

I nod.

The policeman comes to stand next to the para-medic. 'So lucky you girls found her. She'd be dead else, frozen stiff on a night like this. Or the animals – you know.'

'Cats?' says the paramedic, shaking his head.

I think of the dark, the frost, and remember the foxes living in the bank on The Tyning, and shiver.

'I wonder what happened to the mother?' I ask. 'What did she think was going to happen?'

The three wise men nod and sip their tea and mutter and I suspect I'm not the only person wondering about the cold and the dark and the animals.

Hours later, when the baby has gone with a nurse in an ambulance, and the policeman and paramedic have drunk all our tea and eaten all our biscuits, Dad and Eden and I sit on the sofa together and watch *Les Misérables*. It's our fall-back movie. When everything goes wrong, when stuff's too much, we watch it and we all cry.

We're a family of criers and Dad's the worst. He cries at anything. He cries at sad things and at happy things and sometimes it's difficult to work out why he's doing it at all. Tonight he cries from the beginning to the end of the movie.

Afterwards, I repack my school bag, stuff my PE kit in the dirty clothes basket and sit on the toilet seat to brush my teeth. Eden barges into the bathroom and starts brushing her teeth and we stare at each other in the mirror, white bubbles spewing from both our mouths.

We look the same. Both with mousy hair and grey eyes. We have round faces, although Eden actually has cheekbones. Not like Angelina Jolie, but cheekbones all the same. At the beginning of Christmas, Eden tried to change things by dying her hair with henna. But she did it really badly, just blocking the bath plug and dying her ears brown. What remained has mostly washed out although the bathroom light picks out copper strands, and it makes her look more exotic.

Neither of us look a bit like Dad. He's tall and narrow.

Or Mum; she's brown and sleek.

Eden spits into the basin and rinses her toothbrush. 'Are those my pyjamas?' she says in the end. She dashes out of the bathroom before I even have a chance to answer.

'No,' I shout to an empty landing. 'I rescued them from the recycling – they're mine now.'

She steps back and turns to face me, her face shiny

28

with creams. 'Did you tell Dad about the purse?'

I'd forgotten about the purse. It seems like weeks ago. I shake my head. 'I'll tell him now.'

I slip back down the stairs. Dad's by the woodburner, the television news on. His iPad on his lap.

'Dad,' I say, sitting next to him on the sofa.

'Shhh,' he holds up his finger.

'Police are anxious to trace the mother of a baby found in a bus shelter in Highbury Upton earlier today. The baby is thought to have been born some-time this morning, but sources say that it did not seem to have had a hospital birth. They are concerned about the health of the mother, that she may need medical attention, and would like her to get in touch with her local hospital, or ring Sowerbridge police as soon as possible . . .'

Dad relaxes.

We both stare at the telly. The next item is about refugees, and we sit through it in silence.

'I thought she might have come forward,' I say. 'You know, by now – it's been six hours.'

'Hmmm,' he says. 'I suppose I did too.'

'Was I right to bring her home?'

'I'm sure you were,' he says, putting his arm around my shoulders. 'I know it's harder for the scene of crime people, but for the baby's sake. You definitely did the right thing.'

We watch some people wading through mud on the telly.

'I just don't understand it, Dad.'

'What?'

'How could anyone leave a baby outside on possibly the coldest night of the year? Here – in this village? I mean, we got off the school bus in the lane – not even at the bus shelter – what would have happened if we hadn't walked home the way we did? The village is hardly busy.'

Dad shrugs. 'Perhaps the mother knew what time the school bus arrived and that there would always be someone getting off it. The regular bus is more random.'

'But if Eden and I hadn't heard her – and we wouldn't have done if that tractor hadn't beaten us to the top of the hill, if we'd walked with it all the way, we'd never have heard her, and . . . she would have died, wouldn't she? She'd have frozen to death.'

'Possibly.'

'No – she would, because the next person through would be someone wandering up to the pub, at six – that's two hours later. She couldn't possibly have survived two hours. She didn't even have a blanket. Just a crisp box.' The anger's making me talk too much, say too much, but I can't stop it. 'A crisp box, Dad – I mean, what kind of home is that?'

'I think someone must have been very desperate.'

'But what about the baby? She couldn't go anywhere, she was completely vulnerable. I keep thinking about the cold and her being left on the floor, not even on the bench, 'I don't care how desperate they were – it's only one stage off murder. In fact, it is almost murder, isn't it?' The words are bundling up to get out. 'And what about foxes?'

'Don't,' says Dad. 'Don't think about foxes. Don't think about what could have happened. Think about what did happen. You came, Eden came, you rescued her, and now, she'll be taken in by someone who will love her. Parents who will want her, cherish her.'

'Or she'll end up in a children's home?'

Dad shakes his head. 'It's not all Tracy Beaker out there. We don't know that. We don't know anything.'

'But that's what happens to babies.'

'Oh, Amy,' Dad slaps the arm of the sofa in an almost cross way. 'People's reasons for doing things aren't always straightforward. We don't know the whole story.' He slows down. 'Actually, we don't know any of the story. And we have no idea what'll happen to her, but you did what you could; we did what we could.' He kisses me on the head. 'I'm proud of you, Amy.'

The telly is now showing the weather map and there's a blue -3 over our part of the country. 'Eden wanted to leave her there.'

'That's mean – it was only until I'd rung the police.' Eden thumps down the steps into the sitting room and throws herself onto the other sofa. 'Can I have a hot chocolate, Dad – have we got enough milk?' She examines something on the sole of her foot. 'And, Amy – have you told Dad about your purse?'

Trust Eden.

'What about it?' Dad turns back to me. He looks grey with tiredness.

'Someone stole it – at PE.'

'And the money,' puts in Eden. 'All her Christmas money. First day of term, too.'

'Oh, no,' he says. 'That's . . . disappointing.'

'I think it was Isobel.'

'Isobel O'Leary? No – surely not.'

'Isobel?' Eden echoes.

'She was the only one who could have done it.'

'Really? You *think* or you know?'

'I'm pretty sure,' I say.

'But she's your friend. You've been together since you were tiny. You mustn't go around accusing people if you aren't sure, Amy.' Dad runs his fingers through what's left of his hair. And why would you think it was Isobel?'

'Because – she's got it in for me.'

'Why?'

'Nothing – nothing important.'

'I think you're bonkers,' says Eden, setting off a white-hot kind of certainty that bubbles up through my anger.

'I've got my own reasons, and I'm sure,' I say. 'I'm as sure that Isobel stole my purse as I'm sure that the mother of that baby deserves locking up!'

'Really?' says Dad.

'Yes, really. I just know it. Here.' I slap my chest.

Eden sighs, gets to her feet and wanders off into the kitchen. 'I still think you're bonkers,' she says, over her shoulder.

Dad raises his eyebrows. 'I think,' he says, 'that everyone's tired and you should go to bed now. Both of you.'

Chapter 4

'So how long will the baby stay in hospital?' asks Jodie, as we wander down the corridor together. Normally I'd have been with Isobel until the bell rang, and I'd only hitch up with Jodie at tutor time. But now I don't think I can talk to Isobel and I wonder if Jodie's noticed something going on between us. If she has, she's been nice enough not to mention it.

'I don't know – no one said – it might only be a week.'

'God – you don't have long then,' she says, offering me a stick of chewing gum. I take it and stick it in my bag for later.

We stroll into M3, our tutor room, and sit at the back. Miss Devenish, our tutor, will be late; she's always late because she really fancies Mr Treble in the classroom next door, and she does this stupid giggle as she says goodbye to him. She thinks no one knows, but we all know. It's just that we're not as interested in her love life as she thinks we ought to be.

'Was she cute,' asks Jodie, 'or stinky?'

I think back to the babe in my arms. Her warmth, her strange jerky movements, her wrunkled face. 'Oh, cute, definitely cute. And a bit stinky. But mostly she was unprotected – feeble, a skinny thing in a dirty Babygro.'

'So how could anyone abandon her?' asks Jodie, sticking her gum on her pencil case. She pulls a packet of Oreo biscuits out of her bag and passes one to me under the desk.

'Exactly,' I say.

'You'd have to be a monster – I mean . . .' she shudders. 'Imagine it – you've just given birth, all that blood and stuff, and then, you just dump it. Like it's not related to you.' She takes the biscuit apart and licks the white cream out of the middle.

'Inhuman,' I say.

'Nasty,' she says. 'People like that shouldn't be allowed to have children.'

In the corridor, Miss Devenish does her painful giggle and I think about babies and Isobel and sitting here with Jodie feeling weird. And the angry-sad feeling that I had yesterday when I found my purse was missing comes flooding back.

'We went to Madame Tussauds over Christmas.

Ever been?' Jodie stuffs the rest of the biscuit in her mouth, before taking a small hand mirror from her backpack and checking her make-up.

I shake my head, wondering how the subject had got on to Madame Tussauds.

'It was kind of brilliant – all the murderers and Beyoncé and everyone.'

'Oh?'

'Yeah, and there's like a taxi bit that is cool, with plague people and that.' She adds some more lipstick to the lipstick already in place. 'Was she born in the bus shelter? I mean – eeew.'

Back to the baby – typical Jodie to jump about. 'I don't think so, there was no – you know – stuff. I don't know if she was even born in the village, I'm trying to work that one out.'

'But Highbury Upton is so . . .'

'Dead?'

'I wasn't going to say that, but like, village flower show and that? So did someone bring her from hospital and then dump her?'

'Maybe. She was washed – so it wasn't like she was born in the car and then dumped.'

Jodie sighs. 'It's shocking.'

'Yeah,' I agree. 'Dad says there's always a reason,

but I don't see it that way. I think it's like I said: inhuman.'

Jodie's phone buzzes and she reaches to switch it to silent. 'Did you find your purse?' she asks.

'No.'

She sticks more black stuff around her already eye-linered eyes. She doesn't need it. Jodie's stunning without make-up – with it, she's more ordinary but I know to her it's war-paint. 'Do you think you just lost it? Like it just fell down the back somewhere? I mean, I could search your bag for you? If it helps?'

'I think . . . I dunno.' Boiling hot blushes race up my chest and flower on my face. I try to cover it with my hands but Jodie turns to face me.

'Hey!' Her eyes widen. 'You think you know what happened, don't you? Did someone take it?'

I draw a smiley face on my pencil case. 'I've got an idea.'

'Who – who?'

Leaning right across the desk, Jodie's eyelashes are almost touching my hand. Her eyes, nearly black, give nothing away, but I think I can trust her – even though she's the biggest gossip in the world she's still my friend.

'Isobel.'

Jodie's jaw drops. 'NO! *Your* Isobel?'

I nod.

'Never,' she says. A weird look crosses her face – somewhere between guilt and delight. For a second I think I've made a mistake, telling her, and then I wonder if it was Jodie, not Isobel – and then I realise that Jodie wasn't even in PE yesterday.

'No one else was near me, no one else had a bag with them. I don't want to think it's her but . . .' I shrug.

Jodie sticks her make-up back in her bag and stares at the people milling about outside. 'But why?'

'Why Isobel?'

'Yeah.' She turns and gazes at me through her ridiculous false eyelashes, studying my face. Jodie doesn't often look straight – mostly she ignores the bad stuff and sees the good. That's why I like her. That's why nearly everyone likes her. She's mostly fun.

'I – just . . .' I don't want to tell Jodie why I think it could be Isobel. I don't want to tell her that Isobel had a party before Christmas – with a sleepover – and didn't invite me. She didn't even tell me, didn't even apologise. I spent the evening watching TV with Eden and Dad at home and didn't even know about it until Naomi Clark posted some pictures of herself in Isobel's bedroom wearing Isobel's pyjamas, and there were two others who got to go to the party and stay. And that night I cried myself to sleep and gave Isobel's handmade Christmas cookies to my granny's dog. I don't tell Jodie that I didn't give Isobel the bath bomb I bought her.

And that after the party, Isobel's mum took three people to the cinema, not including me, so I persuaded Dad to take two people skating, not including Isobel. Or that on Friday, just before the beginning of term, Isobel had Naomi, who I really hate, for another sleepover

But worse, I don't want to tell her that yesterday morning, practically as soon as term started, I stupidly called Isobel a 'hateful idiot' in the locker room and Isobel was just there, behind the partition, and she *must* have heard.

'Have you been to lost property?'

'If someone stole it, the money will have gone. I mean, why steal a purse if you don't want the cash?'

'Don't you want the actual purse back?'

'No – it's just a stupid purse my mum gave me. I don't care about her – why would I care about the purse?' I say, pulling the cold hard shell over me that I keep for everything to do with my mother.

'You should check,' she says. 'You never know – a teacher might have found it and handed it in.'

'Break?' I say.

'Yes,' she says. 'I'll come with you.'

But I'm right. My purse has not been handed in. The woman who works at reception and looks like an air hostess makes a ridiculous effort to find it. She looks in all the skanky bags and shakes open loads of bin-worthy carriers. 'No – sorry, girls, no sign at all.'

I'm not surprised.

We sit outside the Snack Shack and share a Chelsea bun. Year Eight isn't allowed in the main dining room at break so we have to cluster under the fairly useless shelter that some architects designed to enhance the school. Today, the rain's coming down the ridiculous chain gutters in ropes and splaying sideways all over our shoes. 'So I reckon the best bit was having my photo taken with Julia Roberts, only Mum said it didn't look like Julia Roberts, more like someone else.' Jodie babbles on and it's only a matter of minutes before Isobel and Ayesha come over. I can't help it, I'm sort of frosty and Isobel kind of stands back.

'Guess what,' says Jodie, forgetting all about Madame

Tussauds and my purse. 'Amy found a baby – yesterday, in the bus stop.'

'Wow, you didn't – really?' says Isobel.

'OMG, a real baby? I'd love to find a baby – how cute!"

It takes seconds for the crowd to form. Half a minute for Jodie to tell everyone a loose version of what I told her, and then maybe five minutes for everyone in the courtyard to know that I found a baby yesterday.

Eden stalks past with her mates and raises an eyebrow at me. She probably hasn't told anyone, but then she probably hasn't got a foghorn like Jodie for a friend.

'In a crisp box?'

'Posh crisps or cheap crisps?'

'Better than dog food,' says someone.

'Only just.'

'Imagine sticking that on your passport – place of birth: Pedigree Chum!'

'Sharlene Bennet had a baby when she was in Year Ten, she was just fifteen. Do you think it's someone from here?' asks someone else.

'It could be one of those people from the camp at Swallow Down Airfield?' says another.

'Wow – was it alive?' asks Oscar. 'Or dead and covered in blood?'

I ignore him. I mostly have to ignore Oscar.

'It'll be sold to Americans,' says someone.

'Don't be daft,' says someone else. 'People are desperate to adopt babies in this country.'

'I'm adopted,' says Cameron.

'No, you're not!' says his sister.

'You found a baby?' asks Isobel.

'Yes,' I say, looking her in the eye. 'But I lost a purse full of money yesterday, too. Know anything about it?'

Isobel looks as if she's been punched. And I know I've hit the mark.

'Have you got a picture on your phone?' asks Oscar.

'No – Oscar – I was too busy looking after it to photograph it. It's a baby, not a meal.'

When I look back, Isobel's gone.

The bell rings for the end of break.

Chapter 5

'Sowerbridge hospital rang – they asked if we'd like to come over and see the baby.' Dad is pulling on his jacket as we walk through the door.

'I'll get changed,' says Eden, taking the stairs two at a time.

The hospital is huge and we can't find anywhere to park. Dad drives this stupid great car because he has to get stupid great pieces of furniture in the back – that's what he does, repairs furniture. He calls himself a restorer. I call him a carpenter. In the end we park in front of the radiology department and walk miles along the corridors, following coloured lines, and going through physiotherapy and the cardiac unit by accident. Every now and again there's a helpful woman in a blue tabard who sends us back the way we've come.

'Can we have a snack?' asks Eden as we walk past the cafe. Eden never passes up the chance for something sweet. She says it's to do with using her head all the time to revise. It's not. I want chocolate all the time, and I hardly ever use my head to revise.

Dad ignores her, which is his way of saying no.

Eventually we realise we're on the wrong floor and skirt ophthalmology before finding ourselves outside a locked door in a wall painted with large undersea things in scary dayglow colours. I suppose they're meant to be cheerful, but because some of the paint is chipped and there are loads of grubby handprints all over the white patches in between, they're just sad. They remind me of the dismal underpass by Sowerbridge bus station. Ages ago, someone tried to make it cheery by painting hot-air balloons on the walls, but they just made it more depressing.

The door entry system is disguised as a jellyfish eye.

'I didn't know they had eyes,' says Eden.

We press the buzzer and wait.

'Yes?' says a voice and Dad cranes over to talk into the intercom, trying to explain who we are.

There's a long pause and buzzing noises and the door trembles and Dad makes a foolish attempt to open it and we all feel embarrassed and out of place, but eventually he manages to get it open and we pile into an overheated corridor.

'You must be Amy?' says a nurse called Louise with

scraped-back hair, coming out from behind a desk. 'And you're Eden?' she guesses.

Everything inside the ward is painted in extra-cheery colours, and there are huge whale women in dressing gowns pushing around babies in plastic boxes.

'She's in here,' says Louise, whisking us through yet another coded doorway. 'She's the baby on the right – at the end.' We stand outside a glass room with six babies inside.

I thought babies had soft things round them, but these ones seem to lie on their backs in rows as if they were strawberries in a supermarket. Some of the babies are tiny, and some of them have pipes up their noses and plugged into their tiny hands.

'Oh,' says Eden. I understand what she means. It feels all wrong. All tubey and hard.

'Stay here,' orders Louise. She goes in and whisks out our baby, who thankfully isn't wired into anything and, compared to some of the others, looks almost big. With ease, Louise wraps the baby in a white blanket and comes back to meet us. 'Here,' she says. 'Meet Baby Upton. We named her after your village, but decided "Highbury" was a bit much.'

'She's yellow!' says Eden. 'She wasn't yellow when we found her.'

I reach out, and Louise places the baby in my arms. She feels right, as if she belongs there. Still tiny and frail, but familiar. 'She is yellow,' I say.

'It's just jaundice, nothing to worry about – some babies get it for a while.'

'Why hasn't she got a proper name yet?' asks Eden.

'Oh – we're still arguing about that,' laughs Louise. 'She'll get a proper name, but meanwhile we have to identify her somehow. Baby 20078 doesn't really trip off the tongue.'

'Why's she in one of those boxes?' I ask. 'She looks like a ready meal.'

Louise laughs. 'This is the Special Care Baby Unit – there's the jaundice, and she was probably premature – not much, or her mother had some kind of malnutrition, as she's underweight, so we want to keep an eye on her. Make sure she's in robust health before she moves on.'

Dad leans in towards me, his finger reaching into the baby's hand. 'No sign of the mother, then?' he asks. 'Let Eden have a hold,' he says to me. 'If she wants to.'

Eden reaches for the baby and holds her almost upright, so that the tiny head bobs in the crook of Eden's neck. Dad puts his hand at the back of the baby's head. 'Careful,' he says, as if the baby was our precious thing, not from out of the blue.

The nurse shakes her head. 'She wasn't born in hospital – we know that, so we've nothing to go on. I don't know if the police have found anything out, that's not really our job.'

'So what will happen to her?' asks Dad, peering at the baby's closed eyes.

'We'll keep her for a while – until she starts to put on weight. Then they'll find her a suitable foster family. They're already looking.'

'Who will get to foster her?' I ask.

'Oh – I don't know, Social Services will sort all that out. Our job is to make sure she's healthy.'

Once again I fantasise about us having a little sister. Bringing her up in our warm cottage, teaching her to walk and talk and run. Giving her hugs. I look up at Dad, but he's not falling for it. He's gazing at Eden and the baby.

We all stand in silence.

'Lovely,' says the nurse. 'Isn't she?'

'Can I hold her one more time before we go?' I ask.

'Of course,' says Louise, handing her over.

Once again, the baby curls in towards me and although she's really fragile, she feels right, as if we

47

fit together. I can't quite imagine her with strangers, and I don't like thinking of her on her own.

'So we can visit her again?' asks Eden.

'Yes, yes – for quite a while, I think. She's a skinny little creature; it will take us a while to feed her up. Oh,' says Louise, looking at a buzzing thing at her waist. 'The photographer's here – would you mind, Amy? Eden? And Dad, if you like – they'd love to take a picture of you all – it helps broadcast the story.'

A sweaty man in a checked shirt and with a ridiculously large camera slung around his neck rushes into the lobby. He spots us immediately, and an artificial smile of enthusiasm fixes on his face.

'Amy – Eden – how lovely to meet you – now, do you think you could both hold the baby? And smile, girls, smile for the camera. OK?'

Chapter 6

On the way home in the car I sit in the back, staring out at the moon. The same moon I saw yesterday before I found the baby.

'Little sweetie,' says Dad, as we leave the lights of Sowerbridge behind and plunge into the dark lanes.

'Couldn't we foster her, Dad?' says Eden. 'Please?'

There's a really long silence in which I'm really hoping he'll say yes.

'No – I'm too old; you're too young. We're already short of a mother. It would be lovely, but no.'

I don't say anything. I'm not really surprised but a little grey flag of disappointment raises itself in the back of my mind.

It mingles with my discomfort about Isobel that's been hanging around all afternoon. If she did take my purse, then it's probably the worst betrayal of my entire life. And, Dad told me not to do anything hasty – but that is exactly what I ended up doing. I basically accused her right there, in front of everyone. And I still feel furious with her, but also with myself for doing it. I'm sure I'm right, but even so.

It's confusing.

The moon swings around to the back window and I tilt my head on the top of the seat so that I can stare up at it. It hangs between the lines on the heated rear window. A little fatter than yesterday. Like our baby.

I think about her in her plastic box. Her crisp box too, and I wonder what it would be like to have such an unknown past. No parents, no place of birth. And I think about what I have. I have Dad. To a certain extent I have Mum but since she ran off with Alex the builder she's been busy with a new bunch of children in Australia, so she's a Skype mum – but it doesn't matter because Dad is Mum and Dad.

Instead of a box, I also have the cradle Eden and I both slept in. I have the house I was born in. The bed I was born on. I have Zelda, Dad's mum. And Aunty May and her toddlers, Jack and Daisy. I have this village – Les-the-sheep, (he's not a sheep, he's a shepherd), the theatre people next door, the fields, the woods – everything that tells me that I come from here.

Will our baby find herself visiting the bus shelter on Mother's Day? Will she be sending us cards at

Christmas because we were the first people to ever see her? The last thought makes me feel warm inside.

I imagine myself as a middle-aged woman, still living in the house with Eden and Dad. I'd be baking, or pressing flowers or something, and a beautiful, tall dark-haired girl would appear at the door. 'Thank you,' she'd say. 'Thank you for rescuing me.' She'd have tears in her eyes, and I'd have tears in mine and we'd hug and it would be Christmas and warm and smell of mince pies and the church would be lit up with Christmas carols.

But I know that's never going to happen. She'll probably be sent to Scotland and only ever visit Upton Highbury on Google Earth, if she visits at all.

'Zelda wants to see you both – we haven't been round since New Year,' says Dad into the silence.

'Oh no,' Eden groans. 'Really? Not tonight – I've got to get some homework done.'

'It won't take long,' says Dad. 'Let's go and help her take down her Christmas tree.'

Zelda's house is on the other side of the village. It's larger than ours, but seems smaller because it's completely crammed with stuff. Stuff of hers and stuff of her parents'. It's the house she was born in and she can't throw anything away. Dad lets us in, he always carries a key, and for a minute or two everything's silent – then Davey, her disgusting dog, scuttles downstairs, sniffing at us and letting out a tiny growl.

'Is she even here?' asks Eden. 'We could just go home, you know.' Eden's usually quite pleased to see Zelda, but perhaps she really does want to revise.

Dad folds to stroke Davey's neck. 'Where's she gone, Davey?' he asks the dog.

Davey sticks out his tongue and waggles his tail in reply.

The house smells faintly of artificial flowers, and I wander into the kitchen to see what Zelda's been up to. Davey trots alongside me. A random selection of dusty perfume bottles stand in a group. All different sizes, some frosted, some shaped. Mostly with dregs of amber coating their insides.

'Been sorting the bathroom cupboard – getting rid of this lot,' Zelda says, coming down the stairs, rubber gloves on and clutching a dustbin full of tubes and bottles. 'New Year's resolution and all that – get rid of stuff – although the perfume bottles are rather pretty. Would either of you like them – put them in your window? Anyway –' She kisses the air on either side of my face, does the same to Eden and Dad, strips off the rubber gloves and unties her apron.

Underneath, she's perfectly dressed. Zelda is always perfectly dressed. She's not like a granny. Not a wrinkle, not a limp, not even a pair of glasses. She doesn't look that much older than Dad.

'Darlings, darlings, how lovely to see you – a drink, Martin?' she turns to Dad, dishing out a massive white-toothed smile.

'Not here for long,' says Dad. 'Eden's got to get on with revision.'

'Oh, have you, darling?' Zelda's face falls into a pout. 'What a pity.' She swings around and gets two glasses out of a cupboard, a bottle from the fridge and starts pouring.

Eden sighs. Zelda always ignores the rules. She's built like that. Dad describes it as Zelda's 'inborn resistance to authority'.

It's kind of fun. But it's also kind of annoying.

For example, the granny thing. I call her Zelda, I've always called her Zelda; Dad does too. I suppose not being called 'Granny' or 'Mum' makes her feel young, cool – but actually, to me it makes her seem a bit desperate.

I check my phone. 7.25. We haven't even had supper yet and I'm starving.

'We thought we could help you take down the

Christmas tree,' says Dad. 'As it's Twelfth-night. Just for ten minutes. Girls . . . ?' Dad finds a cardboard box and we carefully remove the decorations and pack them away. The tree gives up its needles with the baubles, and our feet go softly green while he chats to Zelda. All the while Davey sits next to me, waiting for some unknown treat from the tree, breathing heavy dog breaths over the box.

The decorations are random and they mostly have stories. Seven ancient glass balls that she picked up in the flea market in Paris when she was on her honeymoon. Two corn-dolly horses from a Christmas in Wales. Three broken dough mice from the WI. Two elephants and a peacock from India. Three German Father Christmasses in various stages of disintegration, and a load of tinsel from the Woolworths closing-down sale.

Zelda throws herself into a chair and crosses her legs luxuriously. 'And how are my favourite grandchildren?'

I wait for Eden to answer. I can't think how to mention the baby without sounding too excited and I don't want Zelda to get all enthusiastic and involved. 'I've got three weeks before the mock exams,' she starts.

I take some tiny figures from the tree. Dad made them when he was a kid from tiny rolls of coloured paper. The figures sit in a matchbox and they've always fascinated me because they're a perfect family – two adults and two children, and they're all smiling at each other. It's as if Dad made a proper family because all he had was his mum. Wrapping the matchbox in tinsel I drop it in with the other decorations.

'And you've worked really hard already,' says Dad. 'She has, haven't you, Eden?'

Eden shoots me a warning look. I know that the hours spent 'revising' have actually been spent watching hundreds of films in fifteen-minute chunks on YouTube.

'Er – yes,' says Eden, but Zelda isn't really listening. She's staring at the almost naked tree. 'So sad,' she says. 'Christmas trees after Christmas are like broken toys, aren't they?'

'I could burn it,' says Dad. 'Does that make it less sad?'

'I don't mind,' Zelda says, slurping some wine. 'Whatever's most eco. I just hate seeing them bald and dumped all over the village waiting for the green bin men to take them away.'

When Dad takes the tree out of the back door it pings needles everywhere, and an icy wind blasts into the house, whirling them around on the floor. Davey staggers over and chases them until they stop.

'So – Amy, sweetie, what's been going on in your world?'

Eden stares at me, willing me to tell the story.

'I found a baby.'

'Sorry?' chokes Zelda, spilling wine on her beige cardigan. 'Did I hear that right?'

'I found a baby, yesterday – in the bus shelter.'

'God,' says Zelda. She gets up from her chair and rushes over to the sink, dabbing at herself. 'Start again, darling – you say you found a baby? A baby what?'

'A baby human,' I say. 'A little girl. They've called her baby Upton and she's only about two days old.'

Zelda stays over by the sink in the shadows, turning the tap on and off and faffing with tea-towels. 'How extraordinary,' she says.

'And she's underweight, so they're keeping her in an incubator. And the police came – and a paramedic – and they said she would have frozen to death if we hadn't found her.'

'I suppose she would have,' says Zelda. 'Oh – Martin, you made me jump.'

Ducking his head through the doorway, Dad comes back in, bringing another icy blast with him. 'Amy telling you about her baby?' he says. 'Remarkable, isn't it? I know babies were commonly abandoned in the nineteenth century, that's why the Foundling Hospital was formed, but now – in the twentieth century, I mean . . .'

'Twenty-first,' butts in Eden.

'Yeah,' I say. 'Why would you even think about dumping a baby?'

'Goodness,' says Zelda, opening the fridge. 'What excitement.'

'I want to find the mother,' I say, surprising myself.

'How?' asks Eden.

'I don't know,' I say. 'But I just do. I want to find the mother and show her the baby, and make her love it.'

'Gosh,' says Zelda.

'Good luck,' says Eden.

Eden says she really wants to revise, and we head home.

Dad cooks and I turn on the laptop and settle down at the kitchen table to see if I can find anything about baby Upton.

I type in 'bus stop baby' and get a song by some long dead bloke and the story of a woman who gave birth in a phone box.

Then I try 'Highbury Upton, baby', and get Louise the nurse, and Sergeant Harding and the tiny crumpled face of the baby herself. I read the story again, even though I know it, vaguely hoping that it will tell me something I don't already know. Give me a clue. But they haven't got our pictures up yet and there's nothing new.

Then I Google 'Abandoned Babies UK'.

And get loads.

And loads.

Babies in airports, in phone boxes, in bins.

Babies living.

Babies dead.

Babies who have since grown up and had their own children.

Forty-nine of them abandoned in 2005.

There's a whole essay in a newspaper about a university lecturer who finds a baby in a phone box on Christmas Eve. I read one account of a middle-aged man who still has the knitted cardigan he was found with. Dad is looking over my shoulder. 'Poor bloke,' he says.

'But there are so many of them,' I say, appalled by the number of reports.

'Each one's a tragedy,' says Dad. 'You have to feel sorry for everyone concerned.'

'It's still wrong – isn't it?'

'Leaving them? Yes, but there's a story behind every one.'

'I suppose so, but . . .' I flick through article after article.

'Are you all right, Amy?' Dad asks, flinging onions into a frying pan.

'Yes,' I say.

'You're not, though,' he says, pausing.

'I suppose I just wanted her mum to come forward, and I can see from this internet stuff that it doesn't happen very often,' I say, laying my head on my arms and watching Dad chopping chillis with precision.

'It's early days,' he says.

I try to imagine the baby's mum. I think she's dark haired, delicate featured, and possibly already enjoying herself without the child. I imagine someone laughing and joking in a pub somewhere without the bother of her baby.

'Are children really that awful?' I ask.

'How do you mean?'

'I mean, do we make life that impossible?'

'*No* – of course not,' says Dad. 'Not really. I mean, I can't say my cricket's improved over the last eleven years, looking after you two, but my baking has. I can

59

make thirty-six cupcakes without even consulting a recipe book – and my sewing, ironing, bedmaking, and knowledge of animated movies, romcoms, and modern children's literature have all matured magnificently.' He's smiling, and I know that I'm not going to get him to say that we've cramped his style.

Chapter 7

On Saturday morning I lie in bed watching the light turn from street light to daylight. There's just enough for the pattern to show.

Dogs.

They're dog curtains that Mum bought me before she ran off with Alex, the Australian builder. Once or twice I've thought about getting rid of them. I don't even much like dogs any more. I put up with Davey because he's like a very smelly family member.

Clambering out of bed I go to stand at the window. Leaning my elbows on the windowsill I look down the path towards the village. From here, it's just possible to see past the Green Man and down towards the village hall. I can almost see the bus shelter.

I wonder how many other places you can see the bus shelter from. Would the mother have watched and waited, to see us pick up her baby? To make sure it was safe?

Reaching for my jeans, I begin to dress. It's nine

o'clock, which is early for a weekend in our house. Dad always gets up before us and he's already in his upstairs workshop – I can hear the radio, and the choking stink of rabbit-skin glue is drifting downstairs. When I reach the kitchen I grab a slice of bread and slip out of the front door.

Fine rain falls coldly on the stones surrounding our garden. It's the most dismal kind of winter weather. Walking down to the bus stop I see Les-the-sheep. He nods a shy greeting and his dog, Beau, trots over to sniff my feet before padding off towards the church. Otherwise, there's no one about. Since the shop shut, the village is scarily dead. I stop by the empty shop and pretend to read the notice about the new community shop opening in Hinton Tarrant but I don't need to pretend because there isn't anyone around to see me. Ambling, I stop by the bus shelter and read the timetable. There is actually a bus due in about twenty minutes, which I already know, but it gives me a reason to be here.

I stand in the doorway and turn a full 360 degrees. From here I can see down to the main road, the full length of the church and the churchyard, the square with ten houses on it, all of whom are occupied by people well over fifty, up to the Green Man – does anyone live upstairs in the Green Man? – along this side of the square, which is another eleven houses. I can't think how any of them could possibly have been home to a pregnant person without me knowing. Back down this street is the village hall, the empty shop, and three more houses leading back down to the main road again. Those houses are too big and too private. I don't know who lives in them, but I somehow don't get the idea of a desperate person living there.

'Rats,' I say out loud.

There are more houses in the village, of course, so I stick my hands in my pockets and stomp around the damp lanes, but somehow I can't match the baby with any of the houses. I can't match our village with baby Upton. It's too small; we all live too close to each other.

So she must have come from somewhere else. She must have come on a bus or in a car.

I wonder if they had a car seat?

When I get back, Eden's eating toast at the kitchen top and Dad's mixing something disgusting in a pot on the Rayburn.

I check my phone. I think about sending Isobel a message. I start to type it in. *Hi there* . . . but I can't think how to say anything without sounding angry, so I text Jodie – who tells me she's going for hair extensions at the college.

Seriously? I text.

☺ *£10 – student* – she replies.

'Zelda rang,' says Dad.

'Oh,' I say.

'She's got a proposition for you.'

'If it involves money – I'll do it,' says Eden.

'Not this time, you can't – you've got mock exams.' Dad stirs the pot on the Rayburn. 'Do you want to ring her? Amy?'

'Do I have to?' I ask.

'No – but . . .' Dad shrugs. It's as close to loading on pressure as he gets.

I delay the phone call by eating three slices of toast and drinking the bottom of a slightly iffy carton of juice.

'Zelda?' I say, when she picks up the phone.

'Amy, sweetness, would you be able to spare me a few hours? It's a project, and I really need some techie help, someone who knows their way around Google – and, other things.'

'Now?'

'Today would be lovely – I'd like to start today.'

Dad raises an eyebrow at me.

'What are we doing?'

'This and that – and chucking out some of my stuff – a spot of life laundry. What do you say?' I hold the phone away from my ear so that he can hear.

Dad nods his approval.

'OK. Be over soon.' I place the phone back in the cradle.

'Don't let her throw away anything precious,' he says.

'I won't.' I pull on my coat and grab an apple, stamp down the garden path and swing left in the direction of Zelda's.

It's not that I don't like Zelda. It's more that she seems to like me too much. She's touchy and huggy and all the things that you might want a mum to be, but she's not my mum, she's my granny, and it's too much. She likes nothing better than sitting on the sofa between Eden and me, but that is Dad's place, not Zelda's. Often I feel that I have to pull away, that she's invading my space – so when I visit her unaccompanied, I feel a little nervous.

Zelda throws open the door and Davey gallops out and in again and bursts up around my legs, sniffing and yelping.

'Down, Davey,' she says, flapping a hand at him.

He pays no attention. Davey is probably the worst-trained dog in the village. The oldest and the worst trained.

I bat him down until he loses interest in me and goes off to chew one of the carpets.

I notice that Zelda's not dressed though, and I realise it must be almost the first ever time I've seen her without make-up. Her eyes are pink rimmed. She does seem older but she also seems more beautiful. Fine lines web over her face, joining each feature, showing her age, like a fragile vase, criss-crossed with cracks.

'Got a bit of eye trouble,' she says in explanation. 'This very cold weather plays havoc with my contacts.'

'Oh,' I say, following her into the kitchen. The glass bottles have gone from the side but I see that she's arranged them on the windowsill – she hasn't managed to get rid of them.

'So,' says Zelda. 'I want your help. I want you to help me with one of those things they call a bucket list.'

'Do you mean like, fifty things to do before you . . .'

'Die – exactly, although so far as I know, I don't have a terminal illness. In fact, I hope I've got a few years to go, and I don't think it'll be fifty things to do – more like ten, even five.' She laughs. 'I might do this twice, you never know!' She smiles at me, her smile slightly sad. But then Zelda's smiles are often slightly sad. 'I want you to help me do some of the things.'

'Like bungee jumping?' I say. A brief and terrifying vision of leaping off Clifton Suspension Bridge comes to mind.

'No bungee jumping, no parachuting, no high places – although I have put horse riding on there and I did wonder about a balloon trip.'

'OK,' I say, feeling interested, but vaguely uncomfortable. 'But why do you need me?'

'Partly because you can do the research on the computer, and partly to keep me company – there's no fun doing this stuff on your own, and most of the people in this village might as well be dead. They're no fun at all. Can you imagine Mrs Cumpstey on the dodgems?'

Mrs Cumpstey is enormous, plays bridge, gossips and wears support tights.

'No,' I say.

'Exactly,' says Zelda. 'I'd rather have you.'

'Oh!' I say, blushing. But I'm kind of wishing Eden wasn't so keen to revise. She's much better with Zelda than I am.

'Is there a list?' I settle into a kitchen chair. Davey clatters over and rests his revolting head on my knee, grinning in a dogly way.

'Not properly,' she says, grabbing a pen and an old envelope. 'But we could start with some of the winter ones. Ice skating, that's something I did when I was younger and would love to try again. You went with your dad the other day, didn't you? Did you take Isobel?'

I shake my head.

Zelda raises an eyebrow. 'Right. How about . . . sledging, skiing?' She scribbles. 'Perhaps we could go to a dry ski slope. Or am I too old? I would like to have tea in the Pump Room in Bath, properly with sandwiches. I fancy a fun fair, and there are people I'd like to find. Before either they or I die.' She stands up, clanks about in a cupboard and brings out the coffee. 'People from my childhood – like Pamela Stanway, she was my best friend from nursery onwards, we both went to The Shambles Nursery.'

'There was a nursery in The Shambles?'

'"Nursery" is rather a grand word – I think it was Mrs Parsons's front room plus a climbing frame in the garden – anyway, I've no idea what happened to Pamela. And I thought – I could help you too.'

68

'With what?'

'With finding your baby's missing mother.' She gets a packet of chocolate digestives out of a tin and rips it open, tipping them onto a plate. 'I could drive you round, or whatever – in return. I help you find the mother, you help me with my list – how does that sound? And perhaps there's something you'd like to do – a place you'd like to visit? Deal?'

I stare at the chewed carpet. It stares back at me. I'm not sure about doing this for Zelda, but then I do want to find the baby's mother, and I suppose it will be easier in a car, with an adult.

Davey lifts his head and eyes the biscuits, tilting his head in hope.

'So where do we start?' I ask, helping myself to one and keeping it well away from his muzzle.

'Back this afternoon,' I say to Dad. 'Is that all right? Would you go around and get Davey – he's not coming with us.'

'Of course,' he says. 'Enjoy yourselves.'

'Tell him you won't need to eat later,' says Zelda, swerving to avoid a tractor. 'You'll be stuffed.'

I hold the phone up. 'Did you hear that?' I say to Dad.

'Tell her to drive carefully.'

''Course I will.' Zelda mashes the Mini's gears and we shoot up Mayfly Hill, squeezing through the gap left between the hedge and a collapsed wall.

I switch off the phone and stare sideways out of the window. It's less terrifying. Even though I can't drive, I know Zelda is a scary driver. Dad won't travel with her at all.

We zip out onto the main road, nestling close behind a lorry. Zelda pulls out to overtake but changes her mind, slamming on the brakes and getting us back into the traffic.

'So exciting,' she says. 'Bucket list, number one!'

Chapter 8

Parking in Bath is less exciting. We have to stop miles away and Zelda is obviously irritated by the ticket machine and its hunger for coins. We rush up through the city across damp pavements, bouncing off shoppers heavy with carrier bags, past the warm pasty smells, through the buskers and the flower sellers until eventually we reach the Pump Room. Zelda's booked so we find ourselves steered to a corner table, where we both have the view of a slightly bored-looking man who is playing a piano.

Waistcoated waiters glide over the carpet, and tinkly conversation drifts up to the chandelier. Our tablecloth is whiter than white, our china sparkles, our knives reflect the fancy plasterwork over our heads.

Zelda looks as if she feels at home. I'm pretty sure I don't.

Tea arrives, shortly followed by a cascade of sandwiches, cakes and scones. Zelda pours tea and I'm grateful to see that I only have a knife and a teaspoon so I can't be expected to eat a sandwich with a knife and fork. I slip a scone onto my plate and pile on the cream and jam. Zelda takes a quarter of a scone, and scrapes thin butter over the cut surface.

'No cream?' I ask.

'I hate cream,' she says.

'Oh?' I say. 'I didn't know that.'

She looks at me through the steam from the tea pot. 'I expect there's lots about me that you don't know, darling.' She smiles, overly brightly as if she hadn't meant to say it. 'And I expect there's lots about you that I don't know. For example – why have you fallen out with Isobel?'

Instantly, I blush. 'What?'

'You didn't take her skating,' starts Zelda, 'and Eden says that you suspect Isobel of stealing your purse.'

'I –'

'Don't want to talk about it now – fair enough. Perhaps I should have ordered the champagne tea,' she says, rushing on, posting a crumb between her lipsticked lips. 'Only a few quid more.'

I try to be light. 'You're driving and I'm twelve.'

She sighs, 'Suppose so – but isn't this marvellous? Isn't it indulgent?'

'Certainly delicious,' I say, examining a slice of

chocolate cake and wondering if it would actually fit in my entirely full stomach.

Outside, the light begins to fade. Above, the sky has already turned to deep turquoise; below, people buzz back and forth across the square between the Pump Room and the Abbey. The shops look yellow and warm, the Bath stone honey under the glow of all the windows.

'So, darling – do you ever miss your mother?' This is what I mean by Zelda being too intimate. I think how to answer without letting myself get cross.

'No – I didn't know her, so I can't miss her.'

'Oh?' She leaves it hanging in the air. She wants me to say more and the silence grows until I have to.

'Sometimes, I suppose it would be nice, but then we'd have to share Dad – and it's hard enough sharing him with Eden.'

Zelda laughs. 'I hadn't thought of it that way.'

'Lots of people at school don't have dads – we're the only ones without a mum. But it doesn't seem to make us different.' I feel myself in danger of getting angry and have to stare at a sandwich until the feeling passes. Sometimes when I feel like this I say too much and it all splurges out.

'That's lovely, darling, so long as you don't suffer –

I'm just . . .' Zelda picks up a strawberry, pops it in her mouth and then makes a sour face. 'Yuk,' she says. 'Garnish, not food.' I sense her trying to change the subject. 'And – is there anywhere you'd like to go? Somewhere on your bucket list – although I do draw the line at rollercoasters – I think perhaps I'm too old for that sort of excitement.'

I chase a crumb across the tablecloth with my chewed thumbnail. I think of something that Jodie said. Was that a thing that people might do with their mums? 'Madame Tussauds?'

'Really, darling?' Zelda's eyebrows twist in concern.

'Well, Dad won't take us –'

'Of course,' says Zelda, brightly. 'I must have gone sometime in the sixties. It was probably worth it, I'm game.'

'Anything further, ladies?' A waiter glides to our elbows, eyeing the splot of raspberry jam just short of my plate.

'Just the bill, thank you,' says Zelda, dismissing him with a smile. 'As we're here, Amy – we could do a teensy-weensy bit of clothes shopping. Just you and me?'

Clothes shopping?

She pays for our tea and then we join the tides of

74

people flowing in and out of Bath's shiny shops. I try to feel as if this is normal – tea in a posh cafe, followed by shopping – but it isn't. I've barely ever gone to a cafe – a pub, yes, with Dad, but not a cafe. For our family, shopping for clothes is something quick, done in Sowerbridge with minimum pain and suffering to all involved.

It may be the effect of mumlessness, but I've never felt very comfortable in clothes shops. I don't think Dad does either, so maybe he's passed it on.

I follow Zelda through the maze. Fearless, she plunges past sale signs, and at each stop she seems to acquire another carrier bag. She's shopping in a serious way, ticking off some internal list of items. Buying gloves, patterned tights, a new bra, a skirt that'll come in handy, nail varnish, before she notices me. 'You could do with some new trousers, darling, couldn't you?'

'These aren't that old,' I say, looking down at my scuffed but fairly new jeans.

'But these ones –' she twitches her nose at me – 'they're so nice. And it's so nice to have a choice when you get up in the morning.'

So we 'pop' into one or two more shops, which becomes three or four more carrier bags. A sweater for me because the grey matches my eyes, new jeans and a pair of boots, because Zelda would like to wear them herself but at her age she might break an ankle. A new handbag because everyone needs a new handbag. And another new handbag because it's half price.

After a while I relax into it. Letting her choose, trying things on, parading outside the changing rooms, looking at it in the serious way that Zelda's looking at it.

'You might think it's escapism,' she says, examining the lining of a three-hundred pound coat. 'But shopping well is an art. Years ago, before your father was born, I did a little modelling – worked in the fashion industry – never quite lost an interest.'

She rejects the coat. Not well-enough made, and I try to imagine Zelda as a young woman. In a way it's easy – she's not like an old person. She's like a young person in an older body.

'So is this part of the bucket list?' I ask, holding open the heavy glass door of another shoe shop.

'Shopping with my granddaughter?' she says. 'No – but it's very pleasant. Aren't you enjoying it?'

I look down at the masses of carrier bags. I am enjoying it. I like to have new things, but I also feel uneasy at the money spent. 'Can you afford all this?' I ask.

She pauses on the pavement, staring in through the window of a shop selling parrot-headed umbrellas. 'I think I can. But don't tell your father how much we've spent.'

I suppose I think we might have finished for the day, but Zelda announces that we're visiting a travel agent.

'A holiday – I'd like to book a really luxurious holiday. Years ago, when your grandfather was still alive, we said we'd take a holiday, a real one – you know, glamorous. Not a sandy buckets sort of a do; something with cabins and yachts and that kind of thing. But we never did. We had Martin, and then your grandfather died.' For a second she does that sad smile, but washes it off a moment later. 'So I'd love to put that right – shall we go to the travel agency? See what we could do? Where we could go?'

It's a bit like winning the lottery. *Choose anything – go anywhere.* We struggle with our bags through the overdressed crowds to a little travel agency in a pedestrian alley. Dropping her bags in a heap Zelda stops in front of the huge rack of brochures and points.

'Japan? Greece, or the Caribbean? What do you think?

She flicks through a glossy magazine with photos of long-legged brown women luxuriating on beaches. I take down a brochure about Egypt. She could visit the pyramids. We could visit the pyramids.

'Am I coming?' I ask, not feeling at all sure about the idea. A day with Zelda, yes. A week? I'd have to think very hard about that. In fact, without even thinking about it, I know I don't want to do it.

'Yes, of course, I don't want to go on my own.'

'Can I help you?' says the man behind the desk.

Zelda throws herself into the chair and outlines her vague plans. The more she outlines them the vaguer they seem. We don't know the timings of my school terms. We don't know when we want to go. We don't know where. We don't know how much Zelda has to spend. We don't even know if Dad'll let me go.

After wasting an hour of the travel agent's time, we stumble back out into the darkness. Zelda pulls her coat around her.

'Silly, really,' she says. 'Perhaps we need to think a little more. It's not quite like buying a pair of shoes, is it?'

'Have you ever been to any of those places?' I ask, feeling hugely relieved that we haven't ended up booking two weeks in Kerala.

'I went to the Caribbean once. With Pamela and her family. My father disapproved, but my mother gave me the money. It was lovely. Warm in the day, raining at night. Geckos and huge strange creatures clambered over our cabins.' She points at a large photo in the window of the shop. 'The sea was like that, the colour of glass. Chicken and pineapple for every meal, as I remember.'

'Sounds lovely.'

'It was,' she sighs. 'By day we swam, by night we were sought after – we danced and young men danced with us.'

'Really?'

'Oh yes, we were pretty fabulous, you know, back then. Pretty fabulous.'

Chapter 9

We drive back, the Mini hurtling through the lanes, hedges looming up before us, engine racing. I don't talk until we're nearly at the village. I don't want to break her concentration.

'Why don't you take the lane past the church?' I say at last as we enter the village.

'I don't like that one,' she says. 'It's too narrow. Always afraid that I might scrape the sides.'

'Oh,' I say, thinking of the scratches already decorating the Mini.

There's a moment's silence where we narrowly avoid Les-the-sheep squashed against a wall with Beau blinking into the headlights. 'What do you know about your baby's mother?' she asks.

'Nothing,' I say, surprised by the question. 'They've found nothing.'

We thump over several tree roots and around a sharp bend.

'Poor thing, she must have been pretty desperate,' Zelda says, at last.

'Pretty heartless, you mean. Leaving a baby out in the cold.'

'I don't think anyone would do that easily,' she says.

'Really? That baby only had a Babygro – not even a blanket.'

'Hmmm,' says Zelda, swinging the car round into Summer Lane. 'I still think a person only does that out of desperation – she won't feel nothing, you know. I'm sure it will have hurt. Like leaving a piece of herself behind.'

'Rubbish,' I say. 'I reckon she's enjoying herself in the pub by now. Free and unencumbered. She's behaved irresponsibly; she has a duty of care,' I say, using words I've heard on the radio. 'And the baby was really young, which makes it worse.'

Zelda pulls the car to a shocking halt outside our house. 'If you think so,' she says and I wonder if I've been too insistent again.

'Was it good?' asks Eden when we get inside. 'Did you get cucumber sandwiches and all that?'

'Everything, we got everything,' says Zelda, settling on a barstool, and accepting a glass of wine from Dad. 'Scones and sandwiches and cake.'

Davey snuffles over, eating something that he finds on the floor in a wet, clunky, dog-teeth kind of a way.

'Worth it?' asks Dad.

'Oh yes, don't you think so? Amy? And we did a bit of shopping – show them the sweater we bought, Amy.'

'Later,' I say, feeling oddly cross at having done Zelda's bidding and spent her money. I open the laptop. 'What was your friend's name, Zelda?'

'Pam – Pamela, I suppose. Stanway – although I've no idea if she got married. Do show them the sweater, darling.'

I ignore her and type in Pamela Stanway. Three come up on Facebook. Two are young and the third is a picture of a black Labrador.

Eden starts to rummage in the bags. 'Is this it?' she says, pulling back layers of tissue paper.

'Yes, Eden, darling – isn't it gorgeous? And look, there's one for you, too – I thought this green would be lovely with your hair.'

'Oh! Beautiful, thank you, Zelda.'

I go to the messages section and open up a new window. '*Hi there, are you the Pamela Stanway that went to school with Zelda . . . ?*'

'It's really soft,' says Eden, holding it up against her face.

I interrupt. 'What's your maiden name, Zelda?'

'Fray,' she says. 'Why?'

'*Zelda Fray*. I'm looking for Pamela Stanway.'

'Stop a minute!' calls Zelda. 'She'll know me as Margaret. I only used the name Zelda after I left home.'

'What? You changed your name?' I say.

'*You* wouldn't want to be called Margaret, would you?' Zelda opens her mouth to show her disgust.

'S'pose not, it's just rather a shock to find that Zelda's imaginary,' I say. 'I mean – I've gone through my entire life imagining you were Zelda.'

'Margaret?' says Eden, cramming the sweater over her pyjama top. 'Margaret's your real name? How could I not know that? I don't have you down as a Margaret.'

'Why Zelda?' I ask her.

'Zelda Fitzgerald – F. Scott Fitzgerald's wife.'

We both stare blankly.

'She was a flapper, a socialite – glamorous, glittery, clever, witty – everything that Highbury Upton isn't.' Zelda holds out her hands as if holding the stones of the village in her palms.

'I get it,' says Eden. 'Like calling myself Madonna or something.'

Zelda laughs. 'Sort of.'

I retype my message, finishing: *Thank you, her*

granddaughter, Amy. I press send. 'I've messaged the one I've found – the dog one. I'll see who else is out there.'

The conversation roams. Auntie May rings up, Dad and Zelda talk to her and I go on searching.

There are a few Pamela Stanways in the world and I don't think for one minute that any of them will turn out to be Zelda's. She probably got married and changed her name. Or emigrated. She might have died.

After a while I look up *Baby Upton* and immediately our hospital photo appears. 'Hey, Eden,' I say, nudging her.

'It's an awful picture!' she says, shoving crisps into her mouth. Reading the blurb at the bottom, I establish that there's nothing new to know. The baby is still in hospital. The police are still appealing for the mother to come forward 'for her own well-being'.

Reading it all I feel immensely tired. Even if we find anything out, the idea of actually contacting the mother, persuading her to take the baby back, seems exhausting.

My phone buzzes in my pocket and I want to crawl off and look at it in private somewhere, but it's warm in here, so I pull it out of my pocket and check it.

It's a message from Isobel. *Can we talk?*

I look at it for ages.

I type. *Not until I've got my purse back.* But I delete it without sending and put the phone back in my pocket. What do you say to a thief?

Zelda's lecturing Eden about books. Dad's boiling the kettle again.

I pull the phone out and text Jodie. *Isobel wants to talk – what shall I do?*

Whatever you want to do, says Jodie almost before I've pressed send.

K, I reply and delete Isobel's message.

'Would you like some prawn curry later?' offers Dad.

'Yum,' says Zelda.

'I'll try some,' says Eden. 'Although prawns . . .'

'I hate prawns,' I say slightly too loudly. 'They're disgusting.'

'Not even dislike?' says Dad.

'No, I hate. I absolutely HATE. I hate fish. You know that,' I say. 'I've never liked fish, I never will like fish.'

The overdoing it thing is happening again – and I don't seem to be able to stop it.

'She's so black and white about things,' says Zelda, what she thinks is quietly. 'Always was.'

And although it's far too early, I stomp up the stairs to bed, angry with her, angry with Dad, angry with Eden and, most of all, angry with myself.

Later, when the house is quiet, I'm able to think more clearly. Eden's gone to bed and Dad's pottering down-stairs. I wonder at myself, at my fury. What's so wrong with spending time with Zelda, being given nice clothes? Why do I feel like I've sold my soul? Dad approves, Eden approves. Zelda enjoys it. But somehow it feels all wrong. I lie on my side, feeling confused until sleep takes me off.

Chapter 10

On Monday Jodie's waiting for me at the school gates when I get off the bus. My period started this morning, so I'm walking really carefully in case I've had some kind of accident. I'm sure I haven't, but just in case . . .

Like it always does, my back aches and I want to be back in bed.

'What d'you think?' She waves her head about. I stare. I can't remember what's changed.

'Der – hair!' she points at her head.

'Oh!' I say. 'Yes, very good.'

'Is that all you can say?' She swishes her hair from side to side. It is, I suppose, longer. But it's also not quite the same colour at the bottom. Kind of red – instead of brown.

'Brilliant,' I say. 'Only ten pounds? Very good.' Actually, it looks kind of rubbish. But I smile as convincingly as I can and swish the extra few centimetres on the bottom of Jodie's ponytail in what I hope seems an admiring way.

I lean against the wall. I so want to go back to bed and I wonder about ringing Dad. Maybe he could pick me up – I could go home. And then I remember he's gone to Gloucester for some special varnish.

Jodie snaps out her make-up mirror and checks her lips, hair and eyes. 'Guess what?' she says to the mirror.

'What?'

'Ayesha's new Japanese pencil case?'

'What about it?'

'It's gone missing.'

'No! Really? I bet it's Isobel.' The words burst out of my mouth before I have a chance to stop them.

'You think so?' says Jodie.

'Yes – God – that's wonderful.' I clamp my hand over my lips to stop myself saying any more stupid things.

'What do you mean, "wonderful"?' Jodie asks, pinging an eyelash back into position.

'Awful – I mean awful, it's just wonderful because it means it's not me imagining things. You know, with my purse. I don't like going around accusing people – and now – it's like having proof, it's just – it has to be her.'

'You mean like, you *want* it to be her?'

'I didn't say that,' I say, shocked at myself.

'I dunno,' says Jodie. And I can see that she's not sure. 'Catch!' she yells, grabbing my hat and racing down the corridor with it.

That's the thing about Jodie – she can go from sensible to idiotic all in a second.

'Jodie!' I call. 'Don't.'

Luckily she throws the hat at Oscar, who hasn't a clue what's going on and lets it slip to the ground. 'Oh?' he says. He picks it up and holds it as far from his body as possible, as if it might be contaminated. Which, I suppose because it was thrown by Jodie, in his eyes, it is. 'Yours?'

'Thanks, Oscar,' I say, taking it back from him and catching up with Jodie. We wander into the maths corridor and Ayesha rushes up to us. 'I can't find it anywhere and it's got like all my best pens and those rubbers that you gave me for my birthday, Jodie – and it came all the way from Japan in Dad's suitcase.' She looks like she's going to cry.

'Do you think it's Isobel?' I ask.

Ayesha shakes her head. 'I'm not sure – she was there when I left the Z block, but when I went back to get it, it was gone.'

'Yesterday?'

Ayesha nods.

'Definitely,' I say into the air.

We all stare out of the window into the courtyard. Masses of people are milling about, but I know we're all looking for Isobel.

'We'll have to say something,' I say in the end. Although, just now all the fury I was feeling last week has faded and now I'm just tired, and I don't feel much like picking a fight.

'Or we could say nothing – hope it comes back,' says Ayesha.

'My purse hasn't come back.'

'Do you think she thinks she got away with it?' asks Jodie.

'I don't know.'

Jodie swings her ponytail over her shoulder and immediately starts texting someone, no doubt to pass on the news about Ayesha's pencil case, but I feel really uncomfortable about it, and spend all day looking out for Isobel. Who never appears.

In the evening, the laptop makes pinging noises and I realise it's Mum calling from Australia.

Eden looks at me, and I at her, neither of us wanting to answer it.

'Your turn,' she says.

I switch on the screen and a wobbly version of Mum pops into view.

'Hi, darling! How are you?'

Skype doesn't do any favours to anyone, but my mum doesn't need favours. She's a good-looking woman, and with her skin Australia-tanned, she looks like some kind of model. Glamorous, cool, relaxed. I can imagine her legs stretched out under the table, crossed at the ankle. Flip flops on painted-toenail feet.

I've no interest in her, and I hate that she wants to talk to me, but I pull up my hard mother-shell and do the polite thing. 'I'm good – how are you?'

Mum prattles and I watch her lips move a little before the sound comes through the speakers. I'm not really listening.

'And what's happened in your world?' she asks, looking over my shoulder as if there might be something more interesting going on behind me. 'How's school?'

Before I think properly I find myself saying, 'Someone stole my Christmas money from my bag at school.'

'That's dreadful. Not from your new purse?'

'The purse too,' I say.

'Oh, darling – I'll get you another one.'

'Don't,' I say, remembering the disappointment I'd felt when I opened the present. A faux kangaroo-skin pouch with *Welcome to Oz* embroidered on it. I'd have been disappointed with it when I was six. 'Really – I don't care about the purse.'

'Oh,' says Mum, looking hurt. 'Do you know who might have taken it?'

'It was Isobel.'

'She didn't! Lovely little Isobel?'

'She did. I'm sure she did.'

'Well, that's dreadful. You must tell her mother,' says Mum.

'It's not that easy.'

'Get Dad to do it for you, I'm sure he can do it nicely.'

'No, Mum, it's not going to work,' I say, wishing I'd kept my mouth shut.

'I can ring Isobel's mother – I've still got her number. If her daughter's a thief she should know, and do something about it.'

'Don't, Mum,' I say. 'Please.'

'But, Amy, love, it's wrong and her mother should know and she should be given a proper telling off.'

The shell that protects me from Mum suddenly slips and I find myself panicking. 'No, Mum, no. You mustn't – it's not as simple as that. I don't have any proof.'

'Hmmm,' says Mum. 'So what made you think she did it in the first place?'

'Forget it, Mum, please.' If she rings up Isobel's mum I'll die of humiliation. 'But I found a baby the other day.'

'A baby? Where? When?'

'At the bus stop, in the village,' I say.

'How extraordinary. Did you find a mother?'

I shake my head. 'No – the baby's in the hospital now. She's OK, but she would have died if we hadn't found her. I was with Eden and we brought her home.'

There's a huge silence, Mum's face twists and with the lag of the line I can't tell if she's smiling or grimacing.

'Goodness,' she says in the end. 'Goodness.'

Chapter 11

'I need to sort out this lot.' On Saturday Zelda waves at a mountain of black-and-white photos that have appeared in the middle of her living-room floor.

Davey snuffles underneath, obviously hoping that someone has left a crisp in the heap.

'Is this bucket-list stuff?' I ask, settling on the floor next to him.

'No, not really, just tidying up stuff – life laundry. Did you find out anything about Pamela?'

'I didn't find any others, only the black Labrador woman, and no one's answered that message,' I say. 'She might not even be on Facebook.'

'No, she might not.' Zelda sighs. 'But I was hoping, with the wonder of the internet – you know.'

'I'll keep looking,' I say, picking up a picture of three cows and a stream. Davey looks soulfully at me as if the photo might transform into a packet of crisps at any moment.

'Sorry, Davey,' I say.

Zelda reaches for a photo. 'Look, here she is, here's Pamela – the tall blonde one.' She hands it to me, jabbing at the top right-hand side. There are two girls in miniskirts. One blonde, the other brunette. They're stunning.

'Is that you?' I ask, glancing up at Zelda's blonde-grey hair.

'Yes.' She holds up the photo, looking at her younger self. 'What beautiful creatures we were. I was a brunette, then a redhead, then blonde, then brunette and then – this.' She flicks at her hair.

'Why so much . . . colour?'

'We all did it then. It was part of women's lib – the liberation to dye your hair and wear as much make-up as possible!' She laughs. 'Not very liberating, you might say. Here's another one.'

She hands me another picture from the same shoot. This time the two girls are leaning on either side of a gatepost. Both posed, both laughing, big eyes, big mouths. Behind them, summer trees and beneath their feet, summer baked earth.

'So when were these taken?'

'1965,' she says. 'I think.' She strokes a long red-varnished fingernail over the corner of the picture. 'Such a long time ago.'

'The Beatles and all that?'

'Oh yes, and Sandy Shaw and Cilla and the Rolling Stones.' She stands, does a little twist and laughs again.

I pick up another photo. 'Is this you?' It shows a young woman balanced on the bonnet of a Mini, her head thrown back, laughing.

'Yes, my brother Johnny took that one. Look here he is, same day.' She hands me another. Great-uncle Johnny in a pair of drainpipe trousers, a narrow jacket and slicked-back hair.

'He looks about nineteen!'

'He was. He wanted to be the bass player in a band. Shame he ended up as a loss adjuster. Still – that's what happens to dreams! So what I wanted to do was label them all; sort them out.'

'How? Only you know who everyone is.'

'If I put them in piles, then you can write the names on the back – so we can have a Martin pile for your dad, a Johnny pile, a me pile, a you and your sister pile and an everyone-else pile perhaps. No?'

And so we begin and I get better at spotting who is who.

'Martin?' Dad with a cricket bat.

'Yup.'

'Martin?' Dad on the beach, tall and gangly and with hair.

'Yes, and here's one of me as a baby – would you label it, darling?'

'Dad and his friend Ed?' Dad looking even taller, towering over his best friend.

'Yes, the pair of them, don't they look sweet? That's Johnny. This one's Eden, Eden, Martin, Martin, Johnny – oh, my mother and father on their wedding day.' She hands me a large black-and-white photograph. A skinny and rather severe man in uniform and a smiley, pretty girl in a very plain white dress. 'During the war,' she explains. 'I think fabric was rationed, so she had a very ordinary dress – I've still got it somewhere in the attic – and my father, doesn't he look handsome?'

I look in their eyes to see if there's anything I recognise, any trace of us, but they seem long ago and far away. Formal, old fashioned, black-and-white people.

'Is this your mum?' I say. It's a picture of two girls and a boy lined up by a washing line in a garden.

'Oh yes.' Zelda smiles. 'She's the one in the middle – do you see? Same eyes as in the wedding photo. That was their very small garden in Neasden in London. Her father worked on the railways.' Zelda looks at it with great love. 'She was one of six children, you know.'

'And your dad?' A young man poses for the camera, in uniform, standing with a rifle. The photo is battered and the corner has gone.

'Dad, indeed,' she says. 'This was the picture that my mother kept by her bed until she died. She loved it. She always said that Father was such a handsome man.'

I look at it closely. He's wearing thick glasses and the uniform looks too big for him. 'I suppose so,' I say.

'Well, not by today's standards, perhaps,' she laughs.

'He looks very serious,' I say.

'He was,' she says. 'I sometimes wondered what had happened to his sense of humour. He didn't seem to have one, but Mother said he'd had a terrible time in the war – she said it changed him. They married before the war – but Johnny and I were born afterwards.'

'Father and Mother. Did you always call them that?'

'Yes, always. I didn't dare call them Mum and Dad. Pamela called hers Mum and Dad, but it didn't fit ours. It was an uncomfortable marriage. I don't think they were ever friends. But people weren't, then. I think marriage was a business relationship.' She sighs.

We pick through the pictures in silence, sorting them.

'There's Johnny on his bike,' she says, handing me three pictures of Uncle Johnny astride a motorbike, his face split by a wide smile. 'And me and Pamela playing tennis.'

'Seems like eternal summer,' I say, labelling yet another picture of a family picnic.

'It was,' she says. 'Apart from anything else the cameras didn't really work when it was raining – but no, childhood was eternal summer. Picnics, beach holidays, climbing trees when Father wasn't looking.'

She picks up a stack of colour pictures. 'Martin, Martin, Martin, Martin.' They're all babies. There's Dad in various stages of tiny nakedness, sleeping, awake. 'Martin and his dad.' A picture of Grandpa, the one I never met, holding Dad. He's tall, like Dad. Another picture of Dad. And another.

'Who's this?' I ask, finding another baby photo, one that's curled at the edges. It's a very tiny baby. Runkled, and black and white.

'Dad?' I ask.

'Oh.' Zelda takes the picture from my hand. 'I'd almost forgotten I had that. Put it in "other", I'll come back to it later. Right,' she says briskly. 'Cup of tea time.'

*　　*　　*

On Tuesday, I persuade Ayesha to help me confront Isobel. It's lunchtime, and we're out early from Spanish.

'OK,' says Ayesha. 'Good idea, I'd really like my pencil case back.' She looks determined, and I reckon together we look pretty tough. We stand on either side of the art-room door and wait for Isobel to come out.

'We're going to stand together – yeah?'

'Yes – definitely,' says Ayesha. 'But you can ask her.'

The door opens, Isobel's on her own and I swing round to face her, my heart hammering.

'Do you know anything about Ayesha's pencil case?' I demand, my words tumbling out so fast that I sound like an idiot. Not the impression I wanted to give, and I immediately feel like I've lost the advantage because Isobel looks at me like I'm mad.

'What?' she looks from me to Ayesha and back again.

'My pencil case?' asks Ayesha, her voice squeaky. 'Did you see it in the Z block after science?'

'No.' Isobel shakes her head. 'Why – should I have done?' Isobel is horribly calm.

'No – no – I just wondered . . . I expect someone's got it,' says Ayesha. 'I expect it's in lost property.'

'Good idea,' says Isobel. 'Check out lost property.' She flashes a smile at Ayesha.

'I will,' says Ayesha, backing away towards the Attendance office.

'But . . . ?' I say.

Isobel swings round and marches off and I stand there feeling stupid and angry and not understanding what just happened.

Later on, I see Ayesha, and she almost ignores me. She's holding her pencil case.

'Where was it?' I ask Jodie.

'In lost property,' she says. 'Apparently it was there all the time. Fancy some gum?' I take the stick of gum and glance at her. I really want her to believe me about the purse, but I can see she isn't sure any more, which makes me feel worse about everything.

Chapter 12

The following Wednesday, immediately after school, two policewomen we've never met come to visit us. We walk down to the bus stop with them, and show them where we found the baby.

'We've been through this,' says Eden, sounding crosser than I think she means to. 'And anyway, aren't we a bit late?'

'I know it seems that way,' says the taller one, raising an eyebrow. 'But we wondered if there was anything more that you remembered about it. Sometimes people recall more after the event. Especially if they retrace their steps, so we like to ask you more than once, just in case. Can we run through what you did that day?'

Eden sighs and puts on her coat. I'm quite happy, I'm hoping that talking to the police will be a two-way thing, that we might learn about the baby from them, because at the moment I don't know anything.

We trail down to the bottom of the hill to the school bus stop and then pretend to do all the things we did the week before last. We get off an imaginary bus. Eden crosses the road ahead of me, and the police-women take photographs at the bottom of the hill.

Eden waits for me.

'There was a tractor,' she says. 'That's why we didn't hear the baby when we went past the bus shelter. The engine would have drowned her out.'

'That's right,' I say. We walked up the hill with the tractor next to us and . . .' I stop, looking into the dark-ness ahead. 'And a car,' I say. 'There was a car – when I was just coming up from the bottom, a car came out of The Shambles.'

'I'd forgotten that, yes,' says Eden. 'Dark – it was in the dark, I remember looking round to see it.'

'Did you get any sense of its colour?'

We both shake our heads. 'I don't think it was yellow or orange,' I say. 'It would have shown up under the street lights.'

'Or white, or red,' says Eden.

'What about the size?'

'Small,' says Eden. 'Definitely not a 4x4. So it was small.'

'Not that small,' I say.

'Smaller than Dad's,' she says.

'But not as small as the Mini,' I add.

'No – bigger than the Mini,' says Eden.

'Anything else about it?' interrupts the police-woman.

I stare into The Shambles. 'Yes, it didn't turn on the headlights until after it had passed me,' I say, 'and the tail-lights lit up the church – red.'

'That's right,' says Eden. 'It kind of shot out of the lane and down the hill as if the driver didn't know the road.'

'Did you see the driver? Or the passenger?' asks the shorter policewoman.

I shake my head. 'No – and I don't even know if there was a passenger.'

'So which one came first, the car or the tractor?'

'The car,' I say.

'Yes,' agrees Eden. 'Definitely the car.'

We stand in the dark while the policewomen scribble things in notepads.

'Did you find anything on the crisp box?' I ask.

'The crisp box,' repeats the woman. 'Oh – you mean the one the baby was in. No – nothing useful. Some prints that don't match anything on our database and that might well have been on the box anyway. We've checked with all the local shops and they had all refilled their crisps sometime in the last week so it's not a great clue. But we're working on the Babygro. We've been visiting all the charity shops.'

'Nothing in the bus shelter?' asks Eden as we turn to walk back up to the house. 'No anything left behind?'

'No,' says the taller policewoman. 'Nothing at all. This baby is drawing a blank.'

There's this choir at school. It's not very good, but Mrs MacDonald thinks we could be good and she won't just let it die.

She's completely deluded.

On Thursday lunchtime, I head over to the music room on my own. Jodie doesn't sing and nor does Ayesha, not that she's really talking to me. I make the mistake of being on time and Mrs MacDonald hands me a load of badly photocopied song sheets. 'Give one to everyone as they come in,' she says, putting on her glasses and massacring the accompaniment to Adele's *Hello* on the piano.

A string of Year Seven and Eights come in, settling themselves on the plastic chairs, chatting, giggling. I stand at the end, feeling somewhere between important and silly, waiting for anyone else to arrive. Someone drops their sheet, which glides across the floor and I scuttle to pick it up before it slips under Mrs MacDonald's feet.

I grab it and straighten up right in front of a pair of legs.

Isobel.

Oh God. I thought she wouldn't turn up.

'Hi,' I start, but I don't know what to say next. This is not the place to have the conversation that we need to have. I need to tell her how angry I am that she didn't invite me to that sleepover. I need to know why. I need to ask about the purse, and I probably need to apologise about the pencil case.

But we don't speak. Her eyes flick to mine and then away and her forehead pinches. I hold out a piece of paper, which she practically snatches from my hand and she stomps away and sits between two Year Sevens, eyes down, studying the words.

I can't see if she's crying. But I think she might be, and for a second I feel victorious – and then I feel horrible.

I leave the remaining sheets on top of the piano and move to the end of the row, standing and sitting as Mrs MacDonald puts us through the usual half-hour of toneless hell. We struggle through six songs really badly and finally the bell rings for the end of lunch, a second after we've destroyed 'I Dreamed a Dream' from *Les Misérables*.

Everyone rushes out except for me and Isobel. I steel myself to talk to her but it's no use.

'Who are you staring at?' she says, brushing past me and out of the door.

Chapter 13

At the weekend it rains and I promise to help Zelda again.

'But will you come and knock on doors with me first?' I ask her.

'Doors? Where?' she says.

'Meet you in the middle of the village. By the bus shelter.'

'Really?' says Zelda. But she does, arriving in a shiny city mac.

In spite of spending almost her entire life in this village, Zelda manages to look like an alien that has just landed. She stands next to me, holding a flowery umbrella over both our heads, wincing at the rain.

I've chosen a tall house on the edge of The Shambles for our first call. 'You surely don't think the Potters left her there, do you?'

'No – but they might have seen something.'

We knock and the sound echoes down the hallway. I imagine the inside of the house. Dark and chilly. The

Potter family have lived there for ever and know nearly everything that happens in the village.

'Yes? Oh, hello, Zelda.' Mrs Potter senior seems tiny in the giant hallway. Despite the rain, she doesn't ask us in.

'We wondered if you'd seen anything the day the baby was left in the bus shelter – anything at all?'

Mrs Potter stares at a cobweb over the door, then at a ruck in the carpet. Eventually she shakes her head. 'No,' she says. 'Can't help you.'

And closes the door.

'Oh!' I say.

'They've always been like that,' says Zelda. 'Try Alice on the other side, she's usually good for a cup of tea.'

Alice on the other side *is* good for a cup of tea, and a flapjack, and another cup and a stack of gossip. We leave with a brown jar of nameless chutney and absolutely no information about baby Upton.

No one's in next door.

Mr Harrison and his friend weren't home that day.

Mrs Book says she's not buying anything today, thank you.

Miss Gupta had been in London that day but would we be interested in helping her start a film club in the village hall?

Molly and Jim aren't sure, so they get the calendar, tell me about a man hanging around in a Ford Escort and then realise that it must have been in December.

Old Sid tells us to mind our own business and that the police have already asked him.

The Chantrys' dog barks. But no one comes to the door.

'We could try the bungalows in Mere Close?' I say.

'Really?' says Zelda. A look of resignation flickers on and off, before she pulls out a proper smile. 'Of course – if you think it'll do any good.'

Part of me feels that this is a waste of time; Zelda obviously does. But a tiny pip thinks that we might just get a clue – some sighting, something, that would mean that if I saw her in town, I would recognise the mother.

Possibly.

We pick our way along The Shambles. It's a narrow street with no houses, just garages, that leads on to a small modern estate.

'Why do you want to find baby Upton's mother?' Zelda asks me.

'To put them together again?'

'Ah – not just to tell her that she's done something

110

terrible? I mean, if you did find her, you might be very angry with her.'

'I don't know,' I say, muddled by Zelda's question. 'I hadn't thought about it.'

'OK,' says Zelda. 'Just wondering.'

We knock on doors in the close, but no one's seen anything. No one knows anything. No one except for Zelda and I seem to care very much. Only in a gossip way – and that isn't caring.

We trudge back to Zelda's, trying some random doors, finding nothing.

'OK – your turn,' I say, kicking my boots off. 'What do you want me to help you do?'

This time, we clear out a load of Dad's toys. At first I just feel dismal, disappointed that our search has produced nothing, but then the cosyness of Zelda's cottage, and Davey's eagerness and a hot chocolate push away the grey and it feels good to be here with my granny doing something apparently meaningless.

'How many are there?' I ask, ripping the lid off a third box of dinosaurs.

She laughs. 'He loved them. Absolutely adored them. I always thought he'd be a palaeontologist – rather surprised that he went into furniture restoration.'

111

Lining up the dinosaurs I find they come in all sizes and colours. Some quite accurate, others just brown plastic generic dinosaurs. I think of Dad handling them. His little hands playing and arranging them on this very floor. My warm feeling gets warmer. 'So what are we doing with them?'

'Charity shop, I think. And the same for the cars. I just want to check there's nothing precious in the bottom.'

She shoves a box of cars towards me. 'He stole some of these,' she says.

'Stole?'

'Yes – I think he helped himself from his friend David's stack. It was embarrassing at the time, but David's mother didn't mind – we laughed about it.'

I look at the battered cars. 'But that's awful.'

'He was only a child – five or six.'

'I can't imagine Dad stealing.'

'Oh, people do it all the time – no one lives a life free from blame.'

'But it's still wrong.'

'Yes – but there's stealing and there's stealing. It's not always so straightforward.'

I nearly open my mouth to argue, but instead I empty the tin onto the floor.

Zelda peers over my shoulder into the tangle of metal and plastic.

'What are you looking for?' I ask.

She shakes her head. 'Oh – nothing in particular. Just, you know, in case there's a diamond ring in there.' She laughs. I carefully place the cars back in, so that they fit better. Like the dinosaurs, they leave behind a residue of ancient crumb and dust.

When we've finished, I ask: 'What next?'

'I wondered about the dry ski slope, but it looks so dismal on the website and it'd be hideously dull in this rain. I'd rather do something nicer. How about Madame Tussauds? We could go tomorrow, go with Eden – give her a break from revising. Take the train from Salisbury?'

I glance up at the window. It's almost dark and it's still raining. Would London be glittery and warm?

'I suppose so,' I say. 'But I have got homework.'

My phone beeps. It's Jodie. *Do you want to come round for a sleepover?*

I almost do. But really I want to go to Isobel's and laugh and eat Nutella in front of the TV and cry at a movie. Losing Isobel is feeling more and more like I imagine homesickness must feel.

'Blow the homework – it won't make any difference. We'll go to London tomorrow but first shall we make

113

ourselves a cream tea?' says Zelda, her eyes flashing with the possibility.

Not tonight L, I text back.

'OK,' I say, liking Zelda's plan more and more. 'Do you know how to make scones?'

It turns out that Zelda doesn't have a clue how to make scones – but luckily an ancient copy of Mrs Beeton's cookbook does. She produces a tub of clotted cream that Dad brought back from Cornwall from the freezer while the cotton-ball scones rise in the oven, tipping perfectly in the heat.

'We'll invite Martin and Eden – they can give you a lift home afterwards so you don't get soaked.'

Zelda sweeps the toys to one side, throws a cloth over the table, lights a candle, and I arrange the scones in a heap. For a first time, they're pretty impressive. I rummage in the bottom of the larder for jam. There are hundreds of jars, labelled by a million different members of the WI. 'Quince, rhubarb or hedgerow?' I ask.

'Oh God, no, there must be some raspberry in there somewhere – keep delving. Go to the back.'

Scores of pots cluster around my knees while I search. The highest scorer is rhubarb, which I'm guessing Zelda doesn't actually like. 'Ah,' I say. 'Blackcurrant?'

'That's good, but press on for raspberry.'

Three jars lurk on the very back shelf. I lie flat on my stomach and stretch my arm in. I reach the first, my fingers bouncing from the curve of the glass.

'Actually, blackcurrant will do,' she says.

'No – don't worry, I can get them.'

'Really, it doesn't matter – darling – they'll be here in a minute.'

I thrust my whole shoulder in and grab a jar, tipping it on its side and rolling it forward. Without picking it up, I do the same for the next two. The middle one feels empty. I sweep them all to the front and scramble up onto my knees.

'Raspberry!' I say, picking up the first one.

'Oh!' exclaims Zelda, and she swoops past me for the second one, the empty one. I see a flash of something dark and thready inside, but she whisks it away and grabs the last jar. 'Rhubarb!' she laughs. 'What a surprise. Now, let's get this laid up.'

The jam makes it to the table just as Dad and Eden crash in through the front door, scattering umbrellas and raincoats.

'How wonderful!' says Zelda, her eyes bright. 'How marvellous – all of us together, the whole family. Cosy!'

Chapter 14

'Oh mercy! She moved!' The American woman clutches at her chest and screams at Zelda, who screams back –

'I'm real!'

'She's real,' yells Eden.

'She's real!' laughs the woman. 'I'm so sorry, I thought you were a model.'

'How flattering,' says Zelda, sliding me a grin and patting her hair.

Madame Tussauds is a weird place, perched between real and imaginary. I can see why Jodie thought it was cool. I mean, it is cool to have your photo taken with Tom Cruise or Princess Leia, but there's something really disturbing about a wax version of Amy Winehouse, all thin and sad and tiny.

Zelda and I stop to look at her.

'Such a pity,' says Zelda.

Around us everyone squeals and runs to take selfies with the Queen, and Rhianna. I measure myself against

Madonna. I'm taller. Eden towers over Lady Gaga. Zelda peers closely at Jimmy Hendrix's jacket and then catches sight of The Beatles sharing a sofa. 'Weren't they cute?' she says.

I shrug. They look fairly ordinary. They've got terrible haircuts and they're arranged in front of an orange LOVE poster that's just horrible.

Zelda stands with her head tilted looking at them as if they were real. 'Ahh,' she sighs. 'Back then life was so simple.'

She moves towards the one on the left, and sort of embraces it. 'Take a pic,' she says.

'God, no,' whispers Eden, but I lift my phone and take an awkward photo of Zelda and a Beatle. She looks silly, and I feel silly taking a photo of it.

Eden walks away and stares at Henry VIII's beard as if it was really fascinating.

We descend to the Chamber of Horrors. Red-lit alcoves reveal waxworks in various stages of grisly torture. 'Oh, it's just the same as it was all those years ago,' says Zelda with a laugh. 'I bet these walls haven't changed.' We wander past more ancient agonies and stop to stare at two dull grey figures behind bars.

'Christie,' says Zelda. 'Nasty piece of work. And

Crippen. Crippen murdered his wife, you know, he was caught by a telegram.'

Eden puts on her really interested face, although I know that if this was Dad talking, she'd be the first to produce an exaggerated yawn. I slip away to look in another cell. There's a man in a bath writing letters, except he's dead. Or I think he's supposed to be dead. It's difficult to tell when they're made of wax. If I've got it right, this model was made by Madame Tussaud herself, but it seems unlikely because she dragged everything with her after she fled France, and who'd bring a bloke in a bath? If you had just one thing to lug across the Channel, it surely wouldn't be a bath full of wax.

'Oh look, another murderer,' says Eden, her voice on the edge of hysterical.

I wonder at the attraction of long-dead murderers, but Zelda seems fascinated by this bit, so we hang around, enjoying a particularly grisly case of severed heads.

'Do you think Marie Antoinette really looked like that?' I ask.

'How final,' says Eden, examining the guillotine blade behind glass. 'Supposing they weren't in the wrong – no retrials.'

'Yes,' says Zelda, running her finger across her throat. 'Pardons aren't much good without your head. We've become a lot better at grey areas since then.'

The high point of the visit turns out to be a trip through time in half a London taxi cab. We whizz through a long, noisy exhibit that twists and turns and thrusts us under the plague and through the fire of London, finally showing us a very lined Queen Victoria in a huge steampunk factory thing. It's kind of whirl-wind and for a while, I forget all about Isobel and just hang onto the taxi cab, while next to me Eden hoots with laughter.

'Tea,' says Zelda. 'After that experience, I must have tea.'

So we find an expensive little cafe that does beautiful pastries and tea in clear glass pots and weird ginseng and green tea tins of juice. Zelda is completely at home, and I realise she's a Londoner at heart. Despite Davey and muddy walks, her real passion is pavements and shiny shops and little tasty things that cost a fortune.

'So, did you enjoy the Chamber of Horrors?' she asks, flicking a green candied mint leaf from the top of her cake and snapping it against her plate with a long nail, before sampling half.

'Yes – but I still don't understand the whole execution thing. How could they be so sure?' I say. 'I mean, it's obviously barbaric – and once you've hung someone, they can't even have an appeal or anything.'

Zelda sits back and takes off her glasses. 'I don't know.' She turns to me. 'How can *you* be so sure?'

'What do you mean?'

She hesitates. 'You're always sure about everything – it's either right or wrong. Your baby at the bus stop, for example – you know that it was wrong to leave it, no room for manoeuvre on that one. No chance of a counter argument or discussion. Am I right?' Zelda's not normally confrontational, but she seems irritated with me.

I shrug.

'And your thief. The person who stole your purse. We don't know why they did it, but they're wrong. Obviously.' She sits back and a half-smile curls the corner of her mouth.

'Stealing is wrong.'

Eden nods her head in agreement.

'Yes,' says Zelda, 'mostly, but it isn't always straightforward. There are many reasons for people to steal things. And it's a difficult to regain trust – once you've been accused of theft.'

'I'm pretty sure that whoever took my purse was straightforward stealing.'

Zelda takes a tiny mouthful of her cake and leans forward across the table. 'I think you need to talk about it with whoever you think took it. Is that still Isobel?'

'No,' I say, too quickly. 'I can't.'

Her face softens. 'I know it's difficult, but you can't let this linger. It must be so uncomfortable – for all of you.'

In answer, I drain my glass and stand up. 'Shall we go now? We might just make the train.'

Chapter 15

At school, the theme is forgiveness.

'Are you talking to Isobel?' says Jodie.

'I don't know,' I say. But I'm getting bored with Jodie's company all the time and yesterday's conversation with Zelda is making me feel all jingly and uncertain. 'I need to talk to her about it all, but she won't.'

'I dunno if you really have to any more,' says Jodie, pinching her mouth together. 'It was ages ago.'

I wonder if Jodie knows that the Ayesha thing made it worse, not better. 'It *was* ages ago, but it's kind of massive. Sitting there between us all.'

Jodie shrugs.

I try to shake her off during lunch, but she doesn't seem to have anyone else to hang around with and it's not until she goes off on her bus that I get a chance to approach Isobel. I follow her across the car park. But she won't talk to me. She shoulders her backpack and strides off towards the centre of town as if I didn't exist.

Snowdrops appear in the garden and the hospital ring Dad's phone when we're round at Zelda's a week later.

'Still no sign of the mum, I'm afraid,' says Nurse Louise. 'But would you like to come and see the baby? She's much stronger now and she's going to be fostered soon. We thought you might like to see her – just in case it happens in a rush and you don't get a chance to say goodbye.'

Dad frowns.

'Please, Dad,' I plead. The thought of seeing the baby is like a little sun coming out into what's feeling like endless grey.

'I could take the girls, Martin,' says Zelda. 'If you're busy.'

'Would you mind? That would be brilliant,' says Dad. 'I've got a deadline with that table.'

We bundle into the Mini and shoot through the lanes. It still looks like winter outside, but the light is stronger, the sun higher. Perhaps even the grass is a little greener. I sit in the back and stare out of the window into the hedgerows. Zelda stops at a cross-roads and three cars pass, followed by a van from a garden centre with an advert for lawnmowers on the side.

'Spring!' says Zelda. 'It feels as if we should be crawling out of hibernation.'

In the hospital car park she squeals to a halt in a space that isn't really a space. It's a patch of muddy grass between the pay and display meter and a barrier.

'Should we find a better one?' asks Eden.

'No – no one'll mind,' says Zelda, sweeping us into the hospital.

This time we find our way quite easily to the maternity wards, only going past the cafe once on our way through.

'We've come to see baby Upton,' I say to the nurse behind the counter. She looks at me over her glasses. 'Amy? Eden?' she asks.

We nod and her face creases into a smile. 'I am so glad to meet you. I'm Angie – wait there. She vanishes through one of the locked doors and seconds later appears with a much larger baby than the one we found.

'Meet Amy Eden Upton.'

'Oh!' squeaks Zelda.

'You named her after us?' says Eden.

'Yes – it's better than calling her after a paramedic,

especially one called Steve.' She smiles. 'Do you mind?'

A ridiculously warm feeling spreads through me. 'Wow,' is all I can say.

'Do you want to hold her? She likes being held.' I take baby Amy from Angie's strong brown arms and this time she nuzzles straight around, searching me for food, grasping my hair. I lean forward to kiss her forehead and she's warm and soft and smells clean and milky.

'Oh! Isn't she lovely,' says Zelda. 'So tiny, look at those hands.'

'She's a good weight now,' says Angie. 'Much better than when she came in. She can make it now.'

'How long before she's fostered?' asks Eden.

'I don't know,' Angie says. 'But I'm sure they'll find her a good home.'

'Do you know when she was born?' I ask.

'Not for sure, but I would say twenty-four hours before you found her. She'd been washed and delivered safely, but not here. Her umbilical cord was cut badly, not by a health professional. And there's still no news of a mother. Although, if she steps forward before someone formally adopts Amy then she still might be able to have her back. Even after that – but it's up to Social Services.'

'Does this happen often?' asks Zelda, picking the polish from her nail.

Angie shakes her head. 'I'm glad to say it's never happened while I've been here. But you see lots of cases in the papers. Or a few cases with a lot of noise – and many of those in countries without health care.'

'I still don't get it,' I say, stroking baby Amy's cheek. 'I mean how could you leave such a little beauty?'

'How indeed?' says Zelda. 'How indeed?'

In the car park, the Mini has a large yellow sticker covering half the windscreen.

'We've got a parking ticket,' says Eden.

'Oh! Blow,' says Zelda. 'How ridiculous.' She tears the sticker off and throws herself into the front seat to read the small print.

Eden and I pull faces at each other over the bonnet. I don't think either of us is surprised.

'Really,' says Zelda again. 'So unfair.'

I clamber through to the back and fold my hands between my knees. Zelda's rumbling on, furious and indistinct, but I don't mind. I'm still feeling ridiculously happy about the baby's name.

'Amy Eden,' I say out loud.

Pulling her shoulders up in delight, Eden turns round to me and grins. 'Yes,' she says. 'Isn't it wonderful!'

Chapter 16

'So,' says Zelda, plummeting down the hill towards the village. 'How do we find this child's mother if knocking on doors isn't going to help us?'

'You said, ages ago, that the mother would have been afraid – what did you mean?'

'If you're going to do this, can I go home first?' says Eden.

'Oh, Eden, you are heartless,' says Zelda.

'Not heartless,' says Eden. 'Just needing to do better than I did in my mocks.'

We drop Eden at home and Zelda wrenches the car back towards her house.

'Afraid,' I say, to remind her.

'Oh, yes.' She stops the car outside her cottage, and fumbles about in an enormous handbag for the front-door key. 'I'm guessing that she might be afraid of a lot of things.'

'Like?'

Zelda unlocks the door. 'Her parents, probably.'

'You're assuming she's young?'

'I think it's very unlikely that she's a middle-aged woman.'

Davey trundles across the floor and slobbers over my knees.

'So, she's young?' I ask, pushing him away.

'She probably lives at home.'

'How could she have hidden her pregnancy for so long?'

'I had a friend who had a baby she didn't know about until a month before it was due. It can happen – some people hardly bulge, and didn't you say that baby Amy was probably premature?'

I don't understand how that's possible. But Zelda doesn't look as if she's making it up. 'So she's afraid of her parents – why?'

'Because, darling, it means she's been having sex.'

'Oh – but –'

'I know everyone has sex, but if you're young parents can get very upset. In strict families it can end up with people being thrown out – or worse.'

'Really?' I can't imagine Dad ever throwing me or Eden out of our home.

She fills the kettle. 'Absolutely. Especially if you're from a religious family. Any religion in its strictest form disapproves of sex before marriage.'

'But isn't that really old fashioned? I thought loads of people had children before they got married.'

'Yes – now, in Britain. But even in the seventies in this village an unmarried mother would have had a terrible time.'

'But it isn't the seventies any more. So anyone could have a baby and it would be fine – surely?'

Zelda shakes her head. 'I know – but I did say strict. Our family – fine, but I bet there are girls at your school who could find themselves living on the streets if they got pregnant.'

I think of the girls who weren't allowed to do the nativity play in junior school, and who don't come to PSHE lessons. There are a few. I suppose there always have been.

Zelda empties some dog biscuits into Davey's bowl and he rattles it against the bottom of the cupboard, cracking the biscuits between his teeth. I watch him eat, wondering what it would be like to grow up with people telling you what to think and who to love. Parents who'd throw you out for making a mistake.

'But in this case . . .' Zelda reaches into the cupboard for some biscuits. ' I think the baby's mother is young, afraid, possibly less than sixteen, or maybe a migrant – because there's another thing to be afraid of, which is the whole hospital thing.'

'You mean she might not be here legally?'

'Yes, perhaps. Imagine you're working probably ridiculously long hours, and you find you're pregnant – no one's going to help you look after the child. You have no money. What do you do?'

I think of the big daffodil fields on the far side of Sowerbridge and the sad people who were bent double, planting them all autumn. The only shelter they seemed to have was a disused chicken shed. Not a place for a baby. 'You dump it.'

'That's a terrible way of saying it, but yes. You leave it somewhere less complicated. Somewhere someone can give it a better life.'

'So you're telling me that she thinks it's in the baby's best interest that she isn't found? That the mother really doesn't want to be found? Can't afford to be found?'

Zelda slowly takes a biscuit out of the packet, snaps it against the table and gives me half. 'Yes – I am.'

'Oh,' I say, accepting the biscuit and sucking the corner.

I can see that she's pleased I'm listening but she manages not to say anything except for, 'Tea, darling?'

Chapter 17

In spite of Zelda's warning I look up everything I can about baby Amy. I set the search for the last month so that every photo of every baby ever called Amy doesn't come up. My picture and baby Amy's picture come up over and over again. The same story appears in all the local papers.

We find out that she will probably become a ward of court, and then be fostered and then be adopted and that when she's adopted, her name will probably change from Amy to something else.

But we don't find out anything about Amy's mother.

'I suppose the police will have a better chance,' says Zelda. 'But if she doesn't want to be found . . .'

I flick through the pictures. I hate to admit it, but she's right. We've got absolutely nowhere and we're not likely to get anywhere.

And maybe it's better if we don't get anywhere.

My head feels heavy, so I lay it flat on the table in front of the screen and close my eyes.

'Cheer up, darling. At least we're trying – at least we care about her.'

'S'pose so,' I say.

Zelda's right. Perhaps it's not finding Amy's mum that's the point. Perhaps it's just someone caring. So that if I ever met baby Amy when she was grown up, I could say I tried. We tried. We cared.

Later, at home, I tell Dad that our search for baby Amy's mother has fizzled out.

'Are you terribly disappointed?' he asks.

'Yes, no – I don't know. There's –' I'm about to tell him about Isobel refusing to talk to me when the door sounds.

'See who it is, will you?' says Dad. 'It's probably Les-the-sheep, he rang earlier but I missed the call.'

I answer the door. Les stands there in his mangled wax jacket and mud-green Wellingtons, Beau by his side. The rain's lashing down behind the porch so I ask them in. Beau lurks in the doorway, a grin on his doggy muzzle.

'He don't usually come indoors,' says Les.

'Won't he be miserable outside?' I say. 'And I can't really leave the door open for him.'

'C'mon, Beau,' Les barks at the dog and the dog

132

slopes in and lies just inside on the doormat ready to jump at any command. Not for one second do Beau's eyes leave Les. If Davey is the worst-trained dog in the village, Beau is the best.

'Afternoon, Les – how can I help?' says Dad, wiping his hands on a tea towel.

'Got thirty ewes coming Saturday – can I use that bit of field behind your ma's?'

''Course – is the fence OK?'

Les's cow-hide face cracks into a smile and his eyes twinkle. 'Checked her out already. Fine, as I see it.'

'Good,' says Dad. 'You're welcome to it. Fancy a cuppa?'

The Wellingtons are still on Les's feet. He looks down, obviously wondering what to do with them. In the end, he shakes his leg experimentally and the boots slide off, revealing Les's squid-white feet, lightly covered in webs of grey sock.

He perches his bum on a stool at the kitchen top. 'Won't say no.'

Dad points at the biscuit tin and I empty some onto a plate.

'Ah – biccies,' says Les, helping himself to two so fast that I barely see them in his hand before they disappear.

133

There's biscuit-crunching silence.

'You found a baby?' he says to the air.

'Me – yes, I did.'

'Ah,' he says. And there's a long pause while he stares into the rising steam. 'I found one once.'

This time the silence is massive.

'What did you say?' Dad turns round.

'I found a baby.'

'Really? Here in the village?'

We both stare at Les. Waiting.

'Yup.' He takes off his hat and rubs his almost completely absent hair. 'Can I have another biccie?'

I hold out the plate, waiting. I know Les, he doesn't do anything, except biscuits, quickly. That'll be why he's waited weeks to tell us.

'Found it in the church.'

'St Nicholas church?'

'That's right,' he says to no one. He breaks the biscuit into almost quarters and sucks one thoughtfully.

'When was that?' Dad prompts.

'What?'

'When you found a baby,' says Dad.

Les sighs and for a moment I think he's actually going to tell us. But he stands, takes off his battered waxy coat, sits and lays it across his knees before beginning.

'It was Midsummer Day. Chalk-blue butterflies in the fields. I'd been out since five, walking and that. Had a dog called Laddie back then. Collie, just like Beau but not as stupid.' He sucks on his tea. Les sucks on everything. He's got cider teeth. Yellow and mostly missing.

'I came back down Donkey Lane, past the narrow bit where the walls is.'

He stops, staring into the cooking steam for inspiration.

'Yes?' I say.

'And then I come right on home.'

'So . . . when did you find the baby?' asks Dad.

'I'm getting there.' Les grins again. 'Gimme a chance. Anyway, hours later, my mother sent me to put those orange flowers on Granny Penny's grave – what are they called again?

'Which?'

'Those flowers, you grow them out on the lane.'

'Calendula?'

'Ar – marigolds. Anyway, she'd died in April.'

We wait.

'So I goes into the churchyard. There's this noise.'

'Like a cat?' I interrupt.

Les looks at the back of his hand. 'Like a cat,' he agrees.

'Where from?' asks Dad.

'The porch. The church porch.'

'I never knew that,' says Dad. 'So when was it?'

'1966,' says Les.

'But you were only a kid.'

'Eight,' says Les, clearly, emphasizing the 't'. 'Or nine – might have been 1967, now I come to think of it.'

'So what did you do?' I ask.

Les picks up another biscuit and nibbles along the side. 'Well, the baby was squalling something awful, so I took her to the Green Man, where Mam worked behind the bar.'

'Bet she was surprised,' says Dad.

'She was. And she was cross. She told me off – told me to take it back, but old Mr Holdaway said I should give it to him to hold and fetch a policeman.'

'So you left the baby in the pub?' says Dad.

Les nods. 'But Mr Godwin, I think his name was, the policeman, was off playing bowls in Hinton so I went round to Dr Gaffney's house. Mrs Gaffney came with me back to the pub.'

Les takes a long slurp of tea. I realise that this is

the longest I have ever heard him talk for, that he's having what Dad calls an *ancient mariner* moment, getting it all out.

'So did Mr and Mrs Gaffney look after the baby?'

Les shrugs. 'Dunno what happened next. There wasn't no World Wide Web whatnot then, so you couldn't do it. Couldn't find out nothing. Not where she went nor where she came from.' He shakes biscuit crumbs from his coat and swings it over his shoulders. 'Anyway – thanks for the tea. I'll run those sheep in that field tomorrow.' And he goes, him and Beau slipping into the night like two shadows.

'Wow,' says Dad, leaning on the table.

I can't say anything at all.

Eden thumps down the stairs and throws herself into a chair. 'What's the matter with you two? You look like you've seen a ghost!'

Chapter 18

In science, we're studying genetics. Blue eyes, brown eyes, all that stuff. Chromosomes.

'So in theory, in a rural area like this, with less migration and emigration, there's quite a high likelihood that someone like – say, Amy, is related to someone like . . .'

Next to me, Oscar reaches across the desk and helps himself to the staple gun. He fires half a dozen staples into his exercise book, pinning it to the workbench. For a moment he stares at it, before trying to dig them out with the end of his biro. The end of the biro snaps off, leaking black ink all over his trousers.

'. . . Oscar, for example.'

Mr Beamish smiles and congratulates himself on his choice of students.

I suddenly find genetics less interesting and check the time. Fifteen minutes until break.

Jodie's off today, she's gone to the orthodontist.

Oscar spins on his chair, falls off and gets sent out.

Mr Beamish draws some lines on the whiteboard and we copy them down.

'And you'll be glad to know, Amy, that intelligence isn't necessarily inherited.' He smiles.

I grimace.

Five minutes.

Four minutes.

Three minutes.

Someone drops a pencil case on the floor.

One minute.

Bell.

I race out of the classroom and head over to the language block – I'm fairly sure she'll just have had Spanish.

'Isobel,' I blurt, running into her.

'Amy,' she says, but she doesn't meet my eye. Two girls I don't know flank her.

'Isobel, I have to know why you stole my purse. And why you didn't tell me about the sleepover.'

'What are you talking about? I did invite you to the sleepover. You just never came.'

'What? No you didn't.'

'I rang, or my mum did – she spoke to Eden.'

'Eden?'

'Yes – she told Eden about the sleepover. Eden said

she'd pass on the message. Anyway – what is this about your purse?'

I stand there, remembering a conversation with Eden before Christmas. One that didn't make sense about 'she' and sleeping bags – and a roaring blush starts in my chest and floods upward.

But even if I didn't get cut out of the sleepover everything else still happened. My purse still went missing. I almost have to make myself angry. 'You took it.'

'I didn't take it,' she says. 'Why would I do that?'

'Because I didn't . . . Anyway, you did – you're the only person who could have taken it. The only one who was close enough to me.'

'Don't be silly,' she says.

I'm speechless. Anger, embarrassment and desperation for a hole in the ground all fighting for space in my head.

'Anyway,' she says. 'I didn't take it – and you're the one who's been an idiot.'

The two girls on either side of Isobel start to laugh. One of them already texting the news around the school.

'But . . . I thought you'd excluded me, and I thought you were a thief.'

'What?' She wrinkles her face. 'This is, like, rubbish. I don't know anything about your stupid purse. I don't understand what went wrong about the sleepover. All I know is that one day I come back to school and no one's talking to me because of nothing I know anything about, and that includes you and Ayesha and Jodie, so I've had enough of you lot. Call yourselves friends?'

She swings her bag onto her shoulder, butting into me, and marches off towards the dining hall.

I stall, blinking, trying really hard not to cry in the middle of school in the middle of lunch break.

It doesn't work.

Chapter 19

'Where's Eden?' I ask, bursting into the house. Zelda's there, in the corner, oven gloves on. Dad's leaning on the countertop.

'Upstairs, doing her English essay,' says Dad. 'Why?'

'She knew about Isobel's sleepover.'

'I wondered why you didn't go to that,' says Dad.

'You knew?' I shout.

'Yes,' says Dad. He sighs. 'I did. Eden did. I expect you did – did you, Zelda?'

'No – I didn't, actually,' says Zelda.

'Well, how come I didn't?' Absolute fury races through me. White hot. I'm not sure who I'm angry with but I've got a horrible feeling it's me.

'I have no idea,' says Dad.

'Did you know that it's happened before?' I ask Zelda, my voice too loud. Too angry.

'What, darling?'

'The baby thing,' I say.

'It's happened lots of times over the years,' she says.

'No – here in this village. Les-the-sheep found a baby in the church porch.'

Zelda starts. 'Les?'

'Yes and he handed it over to the doctor and his wife.'

'Did he?' says Zelda.

'And I wonder what happened next,' I say.

'To the baby?'

'What do you think I mean?'

'I think,' says Zelda, taking off the oven gloves and sitting down. 'That I might need that cup of tea.'

I'm so cross about Isobel that I can't help being cross with Zelda.

'So did you know about the baby?' I say.

'Yes – I vaguely remember something about it. I must have been leaving home around then – when was it?'

'1966.'

'Shall we go and have a look in the *Echo* offices?'

'Really?' I ask, feeling slightly less cross. 'Would you do that?'

'Why not? If we've drawn a blank on baby Amy, perhaps we can do something for the 1966 baby. I'll find out if they're open at the weekend.'

'There are probably copies of newspapers in the library,' I say.

'Of course,' she says. 'Tomorrow after school, then.'

I catch Isobel in the corridor on her own. She tries to run but I block the way.

'Stop – stop a second. I'm not accusing you – I want to hear your side of the story.'

She puts her hand on her hip.

'I don't even know if I want to give it. I don't want to be judged for what I may or may not say.'

'I won't, promise.'

'Hey you two!' Jodie suddenly appears alongside me. 'Great to see you, Isobel,' she says.

'I'm off,' says Isobel and she swings on her heel and slips out of the door.

I watch her go, and I realise that my anger has got confused. It's no longer pointing at Isobel, some of it's directed at Jodie.

'Hey – what's the matter?' says Jodie as I sweep out in the opposite direction.

Chapter 20

It's more than a little sad to be picked up by your granny from school, but I swallow my pride, slap a smile on my face and march over to the Mini.

Zelda leans over and clicks open the passenger door. 'Darling – I've brought us some Jaffa Cakes, to keep us going in the library.'

'Don't think we're allowed to eat in there,' I say.

'Shh –' she says. 'No one told me.'

We smuggle the Jaffa Cakes into the library and huddle around a strange screen thing.

'Sorry,' says the librarian, coming over. 'We've only got them on microfilm at the moment – I do hope you can manage.'

'Mmm,' smiles Zelda.

'Great,' I mumble, crumbs flying onto my lap, but the librarian doesn't seem to mind.

We find June 1966 and trawl through it from the beginning.

'Midsummer Day, he said.'

'I wonder if he means solstice or midsummer. I seem to remember the solstice,' she says absently, rolling the screen down.

The letters are tiny and the photos blurry so it's slow work.

'Did you get anywhere with your friend?' she asks.

'No – not really,' I say. 'But I did try.'

Zelda leaves a silence.

'I'm beginning to wonder if she did do it.'

'Really?'

'I'm beginning to think I was too quick, too mean. I shouldn't have decided it like that.'

'Good,' says Zelda. 'It's important to give people a second chance.'

'Not sure it'd call it a second chance. I just think I might have been wrong in the first place. I'm wondering if it was someone else.'

'Look,' says Zelda, pointing at the screen. 'There. Is that a baby?'

Yesterday, eight-year-old Les Sands rescued a foundling from the steps of St Nicholas Church, Highbury Upton. The baby was handed into the care of Dr and Mrs Gaffney. Sergeant Godwin, supervising the case, said that the abandonment of an infant is a crime punishable by imprisonment. However, he also added that they would be keen to make contact with the mother as she may need medical care.

'Wow,' I say.

'Yes,' says Zelda, sitting back and slipping the edge of another Jaffa Cake in her mouth.

'That all sounds very tough.'

'It was,' she says. 'Back then.'

'It doesn't say if it was a boy or a girl.'

'A girl,' says Zelda. 'If I remember rightly I'm sure it was all over the village – you think the gossip's bad now, it was rampant back then.'

'I thought you didn't remember it?' I say.

'Well, now you show me the picture, of course I do – Pamela must have talked about it.' She sits back and scans through the screens, looking to see if there's anything more.

20ᵗʰ July

The baby girl found in the church yard on 23rd June has been placed with foster parents and is understood to be doing well. In a statement Sergeant Godwin said that despite the child's unhappy start in the world it was likely that she would grow up quite normally.

'I wonder . . .' says Zelda. 'I wonder if Sergeant Godwin is still with us?'

*   *   *

There are stacks of Godwins in the phone book.

I look up Godwin on the internet and find loads more.

'It's hopeless, Zelda. We'll never find him.'

'Oh – we could ring them all up,' she says.

'You don't want to do that,' I say. 'You'd rather find your friend Pamela, wouldn't you?'

'I could ring a few,' she says. 'Perhaps all of them up to – she points at the book. There.'

'OK,' I say and I make a list of those numbers.

Zelda rings them. One after the next, using her best telephone voice.

'Excuse me, sorry to bother you. Zelda Munroe here from Highbury Upton. I'm looking for anyone who remembers a Sergeant Godwin, from the sixties? Not a relation? Thank you so much.'

Considering that all the houses are local, no one seems to even remember him.

She leaves messages on two answerphones and as the darkness creeps in we give up.

Chapter 21

The next time I see Zelda, the daffodils have finished. It's Friday, after school. I've had a silent week of silent friends. I can't help but look at Jodie sideways and I think she senses it. It's just that I've worked out that she could have taken my purse before PE – in science. It all makes sense. But no one wants to talk and when I get home Eden's in a frump about her chemistry exam, and Dad just tells me that Zelda rang.

'I've heard from Pamela,' I say to Zelda. 'She's writing you a letter.'

'Really! How marvellous – so was she the right one? The one with the Labrador?' Zelda claps her hands together.

'Yes, but she barely ever goes on Facebook. She only saw my message yesterday.'

Zelda is sitting outside her front door on a wooden bench. Sunlight shows the lines on her face, her real age, but the sunlight is also making them happy lines. 'Brilliant,' she says. 'Where does she live?'

'Hampshire?' I say. 'Unless it was Herefordshire. I can't remember. She says she'd love to come back to the village and stay with you – I gave her your address so she'll get in touch.' The message had been long and obviously typed on a laptop by a person with big fingers and terrible eyesight.

'Lovely,' she says, closing her eyes and basking. 'I shall look forward to that. I don't suppose you managed to get her phone number too, did you?'

I shake my head. 'I didn't think of that.'

'Never mind, darling – well done for finding her. That's so exciting, and I've had more good news, I had a phone call. One of those Godwins rang back. Apparently Sergeant Godwin was his grandfather. *And* he said, his grandfather had a diary.'

'Really?'

'He said we could come and see him this weekend, if we wanted. He'll be at home all afternoon with the children. What do you think?'

'I think that's great.'

'And you know we talked about Japan?'

'Did we?'

'How about Paris – so much closer. Do you fancy Paris?'

'Why not?' I say, wondering why I feel OK about

a holiday with Zelda when three months ago I would have run a mile. It's the spring, I think. Makes me feel – *Parisienne*.

'Can we go to Sergeant Godwin's now?'

'Of course,' Zelda says, putting her sunglasses in her handbag. 'I'm all ready.'

Sergeant Godwin's grandson lives in a farm cottage on the side of a road that I've never really noticed. A neat garden leads up to a neat house and as we approach the front door we hear the squeal of small children fighting.

'Give it a rest, Gabe.' A man's voice floats round the side of the house. We follow the sound and the children mute the second we appear.

'Mrs Munroe,' says a tall man uncurling from two bicycles that lie in a mangled heap on the grass. He nods at me.

'Hello, Mr Godwin,' says Zelda, hand out. 'I'm Zelda and this is my granddaughter, Amy.'

'Tony,' he says, wiping his hands on his jeans and shaking hands with her, nodding at me.

The children cling to their father's leg. I smile at them; they cling closer.

'Look, as you can see, I'm a bit tied up at the

moment – but I dug out Granddad's diaries. He kept them every year – 1966, wasn't it?' He reaches over to a bench, picking up two thick, black-bound books with slightly mildewed covers.

'Yes,' I say.

'Well, I got you that and 1967 – but you're welcome to take them off – so long as I get them back.'

We sit in the Seven Stars pub, sharing a bowl of chips.

Zelda's got 1966, I've got 1967.

It's a fascinating piece of social history. There are the rural crimes, like petty theft and driving without headlights. And then there are the urban-meets-rural crimes, like people causing fires in hay barns, but what I really love are Mr Gordon's personal comments.

Took three lads for scrumping from Mr Davenport. Didn't do more than warn them as I know G. Tucker's family haven't got a penny to spare. Just wish they'd be more careful who they steal from.

And

Found a woman sleeping rough in the telephone box in Hinton. Gave her some tea and cheese. She said she'd come from Glasgow and she had the accent. Said she was on her way to Brighton. Don't know how she ended up here.

152

He also puts miles of stuff about the weather. Raining, raining hard, raining soft, muggy, wild, kind, mean, clement.

I turn to June. There's nothing about a baby. Lots about a group of lads on scooters causing trouble. Smashed windows and fears about the 'younger generation'.

I look over to Zelda. She's immersed, a chip sagging between her fingers as she eats up the pages.

'You've found it?' I ask.

'Mmm,' she says.

She's obviously not going to read it out to me so I move round and lean over her shoulder.

June 21st 1966

Came back to a rumpus at the Green Man. Les, Madge's boy, had found a baby in the church. He'd taken it to the Green Man and they'd called the Gaffneys. The baby was with Mrs Gaffney so I went to see it and it seemed healthy enough. I telephoned the hospital in Sowerbridge and asked them what I should do and they said to bring it to them. Mrs Gaffney came with me, her holding the baby and me driving the Humber as carefully as I could. The nurses at Sowerbridge took the baby in. It was a girl. She was wearing a matinee jacket and booties in grey, and a hat. The hospital said she was born that day, but not in the hospital as they hadn't lost anyone from a bed. The baby was healthy though.

Zelda sits back. 'Grey jacket and booties, goodness,' she says. 'It doesn't mention anything about a token.'

'A token?'

'Sometimes foundlings are left with a token of some sort. To identify them. Sometimes it's half and the mother keeps the other half. Anyway – no mention of a token.'

I lean past her and flick over the page.

'I dealt with Mr Fowlds and the car licence then rang the hospital to find out how the baby was doing as everyone in the Green Man wanted to know. Apparently she was doing fine and they'd called her Deidre after Dr Gaffney's wife.'

'Deidre,' I say. 'What a name.'

'It was the sixties after all,' says Zelda, wiping her eye.

'Do you think the hospital would know anything?' Maybe we could find out what happened to her?'

'After all this time?' Zelda looks uncertain. 'We could try.'

This time Zelda parks in a real parking space and we walk through the corridors to maternity, with the confidence of people who almost know where they're going.

Nurse Louise is surprised to see me. 'Goodness, Amy, baby Amy's gone – you know that?'

'What?' I say.

'Oh, darling,' says Zelda, reaching for my hand.

'She's been fostered, a lovely couple. A few days ago.' The nurse rushes for the diary as if the exact date would make it better for me.

'Of course,' I say brightly, swallowing hard. 'I was expecting it.'

'Goodness,' says Zelda. 'So quickly.'

'She's been here since January.' Louise shows us the page that says, *Amy leaving*, and shrugs. 'And we did say it would be soon, last time you came, so I suppose . . .' I can see that she's trying to be gentle. My eyes must be brimming.

'Of course,' I say again.

'But it's not about Amy,' says Zelda, sounding all businesslike, giving me a chance to pull myself together. 'It's about another foundling baby who was brought here in the sixties – do you have any records?'

'Do you mean baby Deidre?'

'Yes, why do you know something?'

'Hello, Amy, Zelda. You're in luck.' Angie comes out of the back room. 'We've got her picture on the wall here, look. The caretaker found it a couple of weeks ago.'

'Really?' says Zelda. She looks at me, her face full of wonder. 'How amazing!'

'Oh, yes,' says Louise. 'Someone took a picture of her and her new parents when they took her away. It's been in an old filing cabinet ever since, but Alfredo found it when he was clearing up the store and we bunged it in a frame. It meant more because of Amy. Come in, have a look.'

On the back wall, behind the desk is a large black-and-white photo in a cheap frameless picture frame. It shows a couple holding a baby. The baby looks like all babies. The couple, like a clean-cut couple from the sixties. He in a suit, with heavy horn-rimmed glasses, the woman in a neat cardigan. 'They look very happy,' I say.

'Mm,' says Zelda behind me.

Underneath is a carefully typed square of card. *Mr and Mrs Burnett, with baby Deidre. July 1966.*

'That's what's written on the back of the picture,' says Angie. 'Alfredo typed that out.'

'Wow,' I say. 'Do you know anything more?'

But I don't find out because my phone rings and Dad tells me that Isobel is waiting on our front door step.

Chapter 22

I sit with Isobel for ages. We both sit on the bed, so that we aren't facing each other. Our legs are dangling.

She keeps on sniffing – either she's crying or she's got a cold.

'Why did you think it was me?' she says in the end.

'Because of the sleepover.'

'Is that all?'

'Well – and the cinema that came after it.'

'Yes, but –'

'And then there was the ice skating.'

'Ice skating?'

I blush. 'Don't worry about the ice skating. That was another mistake I made. But you had the opportunity, and your bag was big enough, and you hadn't invited me to your party –'

'But I had.'

'Now I know you had, but I didn't then – Eden and Dad didn't tell me about the sleepover, or at least, I didn't hear them properly and then . . .' I decide to risk it. 'I said something mean about you by the lockers.'

'I heard,' says Isobel.

'I didn't mean it.'

'That's OK.' She sniffs.

'So does it all still matter?'

'No – it doesn't matter. And I'm really sorry that it's been so horrible at school.'

'So am I,' I say.

We swing our legs.

'Sorry I wouldn't talk to you. Sorry I brushed you off,' she says. 'Sorry about Naomi coming for a sleepover.' There's a few seconds of silence. 'I was angry with you – because you were obviously angry with me.'

'That's because I thought you'd –' I begin in a high voice, and she rests her hand on my arm, interrupting me.

'We're both idiots.'

'We are. And I feel really mean for even thinking that you'd take my purse.'

Isobel smiles. It's a funny, lopsided smile, the same smile she's been giving me since we first met at nursery ten years ago. 'It's just, someone *did* take your purse. If not me – who?' she sniffs again.

'Oh, I say. ' Some low life from Year Ten, I expect.'

'So,' she says slowly. 'You'd think badly of me, but not Jodie?'

Jodie again, I think, but I say: 'Jodie? Can't be her, she's too happy to be a thief.'

'OK,' says Isobel. 'And I'm miserable?'

'You're – human.' I pick up my hairbrush and try to drag it through the knot that always forms behind my head. The knot doesn't go, but the hairbrush bounces off and pings across the room.

Isobel laughs, and slaps her hand over her mouth, glancing across at me in case she shouldn't.

But I laugh too, and it's such a relief. 'Do you want to watch *Inside Out*?' I say. 'And you could sleep over.'

Later on, we lie in the dark watching twig shadows on the ceiling.

'Do you really think it was Jodie?' I ask.

'I wouldn't like to accuse her,' she says. 'But . . .'

I re-run the whole day again. Maths – everyone was there for maths, Spanish – Jodie was there, Katie was there, but quite a long way away. And then I wonder if I'm really remembering things properly.

'What happened to the baby you found?' asks Isobel as I'm churning the possibilities.

'She's been fostered,' I say.

'You mean you'll never see her again?'

'I don't want to think of it that way,' I say, closing my eyes and squeezing them hard shut. 'I kind of thought I would – I sort of imagined that they might keep in touch with me.'

'Oh,' she says. I hear her shuffling her duvet.

'They didn't keep Les in touch though.'

'Who's Les?'

'Les-the-sheep. He found a baby here, in 1966 – in the church porch.'

Isobel must turn to face me because when she speaks she's much louder. 'What?'

'Les, the guy who builds walls and looks after sheep – he found a baby in this village fifty years ago.'

'OMG, you mean it's happened twice?'

'Yes,' I say. 'Zelda and I have been finding out about it.'

'Zelda – your gran?'

'Yes – we went to the library together to find out about it. She said she kind of remembered it.' As I say it, something occurs to me. 'Would your granny want to help you find out about a baby that was abandoned fifty years ago?'

'No – but then my gran's about 250 years old. She wouldn't help me find anything or anyone.'

'I guess,' I say, and I stare at the wall, watching the shadows jumping in the street light.

We bumble through the week, Isobel and I smiling at each other from a distance, but on Friday, I go mad and approach Jodie.

It doesn't go well.

'Me?' she says, her voice reaching foghorn, reach-everyone-in-the-school volume. 'You think I did it?'

Immediately I wish I hadn't said anything and I shake my head, hoping this conversation can go back-wards. 'No – I mean, I just want to . . .'

'God! What kind of friend are you, Amy?' she says. Still giving it the full Shakespeare.

'I just need to know,' I say. 'I kind of just wondered?' My voice trails off.

'For your information – I've been thinking about your stupid purse every day since you lost it, trying to think who might have taken it. I've drawn a blank and I'm beginning to wonder if you even brought it into school in the first place – but now you're landing blame on everyone, here there and everywhere – ever thought it might be your fault?'

This is delivered at maximum pitch, in a maximum crowd-gathering position, and brings the entire year to watch the spectacle. They're already muttering. Already pointing fingers. Already texting.

And I feel rubbish.

At lunch, eating a compressed school sandwich where the chicken is embedded in the bread and the lettuce was grown on Mars, I hang around Eden, hoping her age will hide me while I check out the possibility of talking to Isobel. But Isobel is either absent or invisible today and Eden has to go in a minute and can't I hurry up.

Why couldn't I have a cold today? I could have stayed at home. In bed, where I wouldn't have opened my mouth.

'How does it feel to be you, Amy?' says one of Jodie's mates. But she doesn't listen to the answer and I smile, biting back tears, turning towards Eden, who's already vanished. In the end I have to loiter with Oscar until the bell rings. He offers to share a packet of pork scratchings but doesn't actually ignore me. He even tries to engage me in a conversation about gaming but it's pitiful and I feel pitiful and everyone's staring at me.

We have PE. No one partners me. It would normally

be Jodie but she's made a threesome with Saga and Div. I stand on the side of the netball pitch pretending to look occupied by the chain link fence.

'Bethan – can you please accompany Amy?'

Bethan, a person I've never spoken to, emits a long, quite irritated sigh and comes over to stand with me. She belongs to the pretty, clever group rather than the pretty, stupid group, and she looks back at her friends as she drags her feet. They give her sympathetic smiles.

We bounce a ball back and forth between us. Not a word, and I mostly miss the catches because I'm so nervous. Bethan's quite good at this, so her impatience shows – then at last we play.

Although it doesn't get any better, because no one passes me the ball.

Most of them ignore me, but Jodie's actively aggressive, bouncing my shoulder, throwing the ball right over my head even though we're on the same team – to the point where Miss Summers the PE teacher stops and 'has a word' with us both.

'I don't know what's going between you two, but I don't like disputes on the netball court. OK?'

We both nod.

'So get on with it,' she says.

It gets no better, although Jodie is slyer in her sabotage of my game, and I come to a sliding halt at the side of the pitch with a load of gravel in my knee.

'Go to the nurse, Amy,' says Miss Summers. I leave, watching the entire team smirking at my retreat. Two hundred metres from the netball court the floodgates open and hot tears pour down my face. I hate them and I hate myself. I want to be loved and all I've done is make myself hateful.

'Stupid,' I say to myself. 'You utter idiot.'

I try to clear the tears and snot from my face with my PE skirt, but it's made of Teflon or something that doesn't absorb and the tears smear over my face instead of vanishing. I hesitate outside the nurse's door before finally knocking and going inside.

But at least the nurse talks to me, is vaguely sympathetic and removes a chunk of gravel before slapping a huge, unbendy dressing on my leg. She probably thinks I've been crying because I hurt myself and I'm quite happy to leave it that way. Any explanation of my tears would also lead to an explanation of my stupidity.

They ignore me at the bus stop, and I have to beg Eden to let me sit next to her.

And then at last we get home, and I wander up through the village, my leg stinging, and my mind boiling into fury with every step.

'Good day?' says Dad as we come in.

'No,' I snap and thrust past him, forcing my way upstairs to my bedroom.

The duvets are still there from the sleepover. Mine and Isobel's.

Where were you today? I message.

I watch the screen for a few minutes but there's no reply from her.

I lie on the bed and pull both the duvets over my head.

If I died right now, it would be fine.

Tap tap.

Dad appears on the landing. A cup of tea and piece of what I recognise as stale lemon drizzle cake in his hands.

'Can I come in?' he says, not waiting for my answer and slipping into my bedroom to perch awkwardly on the windowsill. He tries to pull his legs up, but then he slides down and folds like a daddy-long-legs.

'Sit here,' I say in the end, patting the bed.

We sit in long silence. I stare at the rug and feel more unwanted tears creeping down my cheeks. I try to think of anything that might be cheery in my life. But even thinking of baby Amy is depressing because I might never see her again.

'Eden says you had a run in with Jodie.'

'Don't want to talk about it,' I say.

'OK,' he says. 'What would you like for supper – I could do a stir fry?'

He knows stir fries are my favourite meal. But I say: 'Don't care if I never eat again. I might as well be dead.' The words come out more angrily than I intend so I pull the duvet back over my head, wiping my cheeks on the corner of the cover.

'Oh, sweetheart.' He leans across and holds my shoulders, squeezing me in that deeply reassuring way that he always can. 'Was it that bad?'

'Yes,' I stammer. 'It was – awful.'

'Oh, darling,' he says, and he strokes my hair and both our tears begin to flow in bucketloads. 'Girls can be so – vile.'

Glancing up at him I see that he's completely melted and I love him more than ever.

Shuddering, I turn to him and sink my head into his chest, letting the whole thing come out. 'I haven't got any friends. At all. I've done a stupid thing – I've accused them all of things that they didn't do.'

'What about Isobel?' he asks. 'She was lovely last weekend.'

I glance at my phone. 'Isobel's vanished. I think

she's ill or something – or moved to Australia, I don't know. She won't answer.'

'Oh,' says Dad, wiping his face on his sleeve. 'That's disappointing.'

I uncurl from his arms and lie back against my pillow. I grab Babbit, my ancient grey-eared rabbit and hold him close.

He starts talking, in a Dad-filling-all-the-space kind of way.

'I called in on Zelda yesterday. Chopped her some wood.'

'Oh?' I say.

'I wondered why she hadn't been round. I wondered why you hadn't been round there – searching for babies or parents.'

'I dunno.' I say. 'I've kind of lost interest.'

'Oh, OK.'

'And I won't get to see baby Amy any more.'

'Ah.'

'She's been sent away somewhere, fostered.'

I lie and close my eyes, and just when I'm on the final tip of sleep, I hear Dad creeping out of the room.

Chapter 23

I sleep most of Saturday.

I try to sleep on Sunday but wake in the middle of the night, still wearing the clothes I put on yesterday. I undress, pull on my nightie and clamber under the duvet. It's warm from where I've been sleeping on it and I snuggle under, waiting for sleep to come.

It doesn't. I turn Friday, at school, over and over in my mind. No matter which way up it is, it looks rubbish. I can't improve on no one talking to me, except for Oscar and he doesn't count. I can't go in tomorrow, I just can't.

I'll have to pull a sickie.

But Dad hates me doing that. He says Zelda made him go in no matter what.

But I can't go in. I just can't. I'll be truly sick if I have to put up with another day of it.

I turn over and stare at the crack of light under the door.

And what happened to Isobel? Why wasn't she there?

Suddenly I'm too hot and I throw the duvet back. Sleep almost creeps up, but I get cold and pull the duvet up again.

I lie flat on my back. Twig silhouettes dance on the ceiling with faint dog shadows from the curtains. Something heavy drives along the main road, tyres sloshing, echoing through the square, and off in the distance a train rumbles through the valley.

My bedside clock says 4.16 a.m. and I'm tempted to turn on the radio for some company. I suppose I've been asleep since about seven. That's hours.

Perhaps I'm hungry.

I swing my feet out of bed and pull open the door. The landing light is enough to get me down the stairs and I just have to steel myself to open the kitchen door. I've never liked wandering about at night – not that I really believe in monsters, but the shadows are weird and the noises are noisier.

The fridge hums like it did in that book I had when I was a kid. Where father bear wants to find a quiet place to sleep. I find it reassuring and its yellow light when I open it is normal and not scary like the creepy fridge light in *Close Encounters*.

Cheese.

I cut off a chunk and slice up an apple and eat them together. A mouthful of each.

A glass of water and then bed.

I see a note in Zelda's handwriting pinned to the noticeboard.

Basil please. Love, Zelda.

Love.

Love?

Halfway up the stairs it occurs to me that Zelda referred to 1965 as her summer of love. That she was sitting on car bonnets having her photo taken like some grown-up model. That she was in the village when the baby Deidre was left in the church-yard. She would have known whoever left it. Surely. Back then, when everyone knew everyone else's business, when the village was full of people working in it.

I pad back to my bed and climb in, clutching my knees through the duvet.

And then I think about all the stuff we've been doing. Seeking out people, the past. Sorting through her stuff, and what was that thing in the jam jar that she whisked away when we were looking for raspberry jam?

And the photo of the 'other' baby.

Who was that?

I wait until six and then I go to wake Dad.

'What? What the?'

He sits up, looking surprised and ever so slightly angry.

'Amy? Are you all right?'

'Fine, Dad,' I say, sitting on his feet. 'I've been thinking.'

'I've been sleeping,' he says.

'It's just the whole thing with Zelda.'

'Zelda?' he says, running his hands through his hair and blinking. 'We're talking about Zelda at six in the morning?'

'I'm thinking –' I say – 'that's she's been too helpful.'

Dad says nothing, waiting for me to continue. His eyes are going from completely asleep to slightly awake.

'She's been looking stuff up with me, she's been driving me to hospitals – she's just been too keen.'

'And?'

'She would have been here in 1966 – she would have been sixteen – just the right age to know the person that abandoned that baby.' I take a deep breath.

'And she's got this picture of a baby that isn't you.'

'Has she?' Dad's sitting up now.

'And she's gone quiet, hasn't she – we got so far and she stopped ringing, stopped asking for me to go over – she's like someone who's waiting for something to happen. Or she's scared it *is* going to happen.'

'I suppose she sort of has – but I thought you'd just put it aside, with all this Isobel business.'

'I may have done, but she has too. Even the bucket list has gone quiet.'

'It has, hasn't it?' Dad reaches for a glass of water coated with dust.

'Exactly,' I say. 'Exactly.'

'She can't just have the day off because everyone's being mean,' says Eden. 'Can she?'

But Eden goes down to the bus stop on her own, although muttering curses and threatening to expose me to the head, which I know she won't.

'Sure about this?' says Dad at half past eight.

'Yup,' I say, and we lock the front door and set off down the path past the freshly greened hazels in the hedge.

We walk in silence to Zelda's. Her lights are on in the kitchen, but Dad knocks this time. She comes to the door, smiling. 'Hello, darlings.' But her face falls quickly when she sees mine.

'Oh,' she says. 'You'd better come in.'

We sit on her sofa, Dad's hand really close to mine.

'Would you like a coffee or something? Sweetie? Martin?' she says.

I stare stonily. Dad mutters, 'No, thank you.'

The atmosphere is thick and hot, but I want it that way. If what I think is true – then I want the atmosphere in flames.

'So.' Zelda sits down at the end, her legs slanted, her hands clasped between her knees. She looks from me to Dad and back again.

'It was you, wasn't it?' I begin. 'In 1966.'

'Amy,' mumbles Dad. 'Don't –'

But I've got the hang of it now. The accusing bit. 'You were that mother – the one that left that child – she was the result of your summer of love, wasn't she?'

'Amy!'

'Well, wasn't she?' I say.

There's a hideous, long pause while I wonder if I've got it wrong again – that I've accused yet another person of something they didn't do.

Zelda bends her head. I can't see her face.

'Darlings,' she says.

That's all she says and then she looks up. She's crying. I've never seen Zelda cry. 'I should – I should never – I don't know what to say. Was it the photo?'

'Oh God – she's right?' says Dad, stumbling over the words. 'You mean I had a sister?'

'You still do,' says Zelda, looking up at him, wiping her nose on the back of her hand. 'Somewhere.'

The silence stretches. I can't frame the words – I'm too angry, too confused. Dad's shaking his head and having a silent conversation with the arm of the sofa.

Outside, a car door slams, and someone talks to someone else and then feet slap on the path. I tense, listening to it getting closer to the door.

Bing bong

Davey lunges half-heartedly from the rug and lets out an almost-bark.

'Oh dear,' says Zelda. She gets up and goes to the door.

'Just the one to sign for and a letter.' The postman.

'Thanks,' says Zelda. 'Bye now.'

Dad and I sit still on the sofa, staring at the floor. Zelda comes back to sit opposite us.

I stand up so that I can't see her, and look out of the window, down towards the church. It focuses my thoughts. 'But how could you have done it? How could you leave a baby on her own like that in the church porch? How could you?' I demand, swinging round to face her.

'Amy, darling, I'm not an animal. I didn't leave her out on the hillside to be pecked at. We put her behind the wire bird doors in the porch so that she'd be safe.'

'Who's "we"?'

'Pamela and I.'

'So you thought a bench in a cold, stone church was safe? She might have stayed there for ever – it's just chance that Les found her.'

'I knew she'd be found,' says Zelda. 'We checked on her.'

'Oh,' I say.

There's a silence. Dad's white. Actually grey, staring at the floor. I feel like some of the wind's gone from my sails. 'But didn't it hurt – leaving her there?' I say.

'Of course it did – it hurt terribly – but I had no choice.'

'Of course you had a choice,' I say, riding a new wave of anger. 'You could have had no baby, you could have kept her, you could have handed her in and told them who you were – you could have done any of those things –'

'No! I couldn't.' Zelda stands and crosses the room. 'No, Amy – it wasn't that simple. You have no idea what it was like then.'

'How did you cover it up?' says Dad, speaking for the first time.

'Pamela helped me.' Zelda sits down again. 'I had to tell someone so I told her. And luckily swing coats were in fashion, and it was a cool spring so I wore mine all the time. It covered the bulge – and then when the baby came, I gave birth to her on Pamela's farm. Straw and everything.'

'Oh God,' says Dad.

'She'd delivered hundreds of lambs and calves. Or at least she said she had.'

'Oh God,' says Dad again.

'And then when I'd had a rest, and stroked the little thing and fed her, we left her in the churchyard,' Zelda almost whispers. 'We sat on a bench. On the other side of the wall, and listened.'

I slide back onto the sofa by Dad. I can picture it. I know where the bench is. How the porch looks. I can even imagine Les when he was eight.

'I heard Les find her. Heard him take her away, but I didn't know what happened next because my parents took me away to Scotland for a holiday. I pretended that I'd got a stomach ache so they left me alone as I recovered.'

We sit in silence.

'For a long time,' says Zelda, 'I almost forgot. I almost didn't think about her. Occasionally you'd read about a foundling in the papers, but I really could say I was able to pretend it never happened.'

'You could forget about it?' asks Dad. 'Really?'

'You'd never forget,' says Zelda. 'But I lived with it, at the back of my mind.'

'Oh,' says Dad.

'After my A levels, I went to art school, met your father, Martin, and married him. I told him, but he never asked any more about it and I suppose that once you were born I was so involved in bringing you up I rarely thought about that other baby. Every now and again I'd see a girl about the right age and I'd wonder, but it wasn't in my mind all the time until . . .'

'Until I found baby Amy.'

'Yes,' says Zelda.'

'How could you?' I say again.

'Because my parents would have thrown me out. Me and the baby. Or, she'd have been taken off me. I'd heard of girls being sent away to strange places to give birth and their babies being taken away. There were rumours of unwanted babies going to Australia from institutions – I didn't want that. I wanted her in England, even if I wasn't able to see her or speak to her. I wanted other people to have seen her. To know she existed.'

'Mum,' says Dad. 'How? How could I not know this?'

And I get up and leave.

Chapter 24

I must walk down from Zelda's. I don't know, I'm not really looking. I wander through the village, back towards our house but I don't want to go home. I'm too angry, with too many thoughts. Instead I take the footpath that goes up the hill, a long, steady, wide field, empty but the grass is coming on, and the first dandelions are showing their heads. On the right, a tangled hedge bursts with fresh bryony, its alien leaves curling through the brambles, themselves spurting tiny points of new growth. I walk on and on until I reach the top of the hill, where I sit on a stone and stare at the view. The view I've known all my life. Distant sheep in distant fields. The trees all spotting with green, the grass becoming brighter and the brown tracks thinning. Disappearing under the onset of April. A lone bumble bee cruises past and the sun comes out, suddenly hotter than I was expecting. It's all beautiful, it's all calming but I'm so hot inside, no amount of comfort can clear it away.

'How could you!' I shout at the bumble bee's disappearing bottom.

A pigeon flaps slowly overhead.

I sit in silence, the thoughts crowding and circling.

All the things I thought I knew aren't true. Everything I grew up with is wrong. And everything I thought was solid in my world isn't. Zelda. Jodie, even Isobel. None of them are who I thought they were.

I've been getting them wrong.

And then there's Mum. She must have pretended to love us when we were little, but she didn't. Otherwise she'd have stayed.

Although the sun warms me, almost burns the top of my hair, I'm cold and I feel cut adrift. Foolish. I feel like the world's biggest idiot and I wish I could see little Amy again.

She's done nothing wrong. She hasn't let anyone down.

I stand up from the stone and start walking. Over the hill and down the other side. Across the lanes, on and on and even though it starts to rain I just keep on walking, my anger keeps on burning and the rain falls harder, trying to put it out.

I walk to Wraxall. The church clock says four and I realise I don't have my phone, and there isn't a phone box. I try the church but it's locked and the closed-up pub opposite stares sadly at me with blank windows. Rain streams down the front of the church, bouncing off the flagstones, gurgling from the gutters. First I lurk under a laurel bush, which works quite well, but soon it sags and the water spouts down my arms, drenching me. So once I'm soaked, I flatten myself against the church door, and find that I can avoid getting much wetter. A spider builds a web between the door and the archway and sits in the middle, waiting for something to happen. I slide down the door, watching the light go out of the sky.

The clock strikes five.

I'm cold.

Cold on the inside, cold on the outside. My knees are soaking wet.

Headlights swing across the front of the pub. Zelda's Mini cruises past very slowly and I almost hide. But she stops. She pulls on a raincoat and stumbles towards me. 'Amy, darling – what are you doing?'

I don't answer. She shepherds me down to her car, which is warm, and I sit, dripping all over the upholstery, gradual steam rising from my feet.

She talks. 'I know you're furious with me. I know you're angry – but give me a chance to explain.'

I stare out of the window, radiating fury across the car.

'It was different then – I couldn't possibly have told my father – he'd . . . he'd – oh!' She shakes her head and we leave Wraxall and slide and skid through the lanes until we reach home.

I don't say a word. Not even 'thank you', which I know is rude of me, but I can't. I just can't.

'I'll tell him I found you,' shouts Zelda. I don't turn. I won't give in and I push open the door of our cottage.

Eden looks up. 'Oh, Amy! Thank God. Dad's out there looking for you. It's all . . .'

'A disaster,' I say, sweeping past and heading for the bathroom. I peel off my clothes and stand shaking under the showerhead until I can get my fingers to turn on the hot water. It burns as it hits my freezing-cold skin and I watch my limbs go from white to pink, and I'm almost angry that they do because I want that anger – I want that fury, I want the cold thing. The uncaring, untouchable thing. But the shower won't let me – it's too intimate, too kind, too warming and I realise, as I stand under the shower, becoming human again, that I haven't eaten since yesterday, and I am all at once ravenous.

Which is not good, because I had planned on shutting myself in my bedroom and not talking to anyone, not even Eden or Dad, but I'm going to have to go down and eat.

Wrapping myself in as many towels as I can find, I pad downstairs just as Dad comes through the front door.

'Amy!' he says. 'Where the hell were you?'

'Why do you care?' I say before I can stop myself.

'I care, I care very much. And so does Zelda,' he shouts. Dad never shouts and I realise that he's actually angry. This is not what I expected. He paces the floor, then slams his hand on the table, looking up at me, his face drained, pale, very old. 'It's not like she did this on purpose to hurt, you know. It wasn't planned – she wasn't expecting you to find a baby.'

He breathes, puts his hands on his hips and walks around the room. His voice drops, but he's still angry.

'She was Eden's age, she was pregnant. She couldn't tell her father or her mother, so she acted out of desperation.' He swings around to face me. 'Understand it, Amy – the world's not black and white, it's grey, it's full of grey stuff. People make grey decisions, things they regret later because they can't all see it as clearly as you do.'

He pauses and sags into a chair. Eden pushes a

cup of tea towards him, he smiles at her and then talks to me in a low voice. 'It's all very well going around being so self-righteous all the time. So judgemental, but sometimes, Amy, you sound exactly like my grandparents. People mustn't do this or that or upset anyone – or anything really! – but life's not like that, it's messier.'

'It is – it ought to be,' I say. 'People can't just go around leaving babies – they're human beings, they're tiny little human beings.' My anger's all over the place, tears mixed with this hot, high, clear thing – this thing that splits right from wrong.

'Oh, for goodness' sake,' says Dad, his exasperation radiating.

'Don't you understand, Dad? I thought I could rely on her. Zelda's my grandmother, she's supposed to be wise. She's supposed to show me the way.' I wave to include Eden. 'Show us the way – but look, she's hollow and fake and not the thing I thought she was at all, and you're taking her side. I don't get that at all.'

I go to the sink, fill a glass with water and drink it down in one.

Dad sighs. 'It's not about sides, Amy. It's not a question of right and wrong – it's not like that. She knows it was wrong. She's full of regret – but it happened. And it happened a long time ago.'

'And actually,' interrupts Eden. 'It's more Dad's problem than ours. He's the one who grew up with an invisible sister.'

'Well,' says Dad, 'sort of.'

The words fall into silence. We all sit, thinking. Dad leans across and gives Eden a hug.

Jealousy catches me out and I suddenly long for Dad's approval.

'So – Amy, will you go and see her. Make peace?' says Dad. 'For my sake if nothing else.'

'*No*,' I say and stomp off to bed.

Later, Dad and I have a conversation through the bedroom door. I'm not going to let him in. He can't bring me round, I won't let him.

'You'll have to go to school tomorrow, sweetheart – I won't be here.'

Oh no. 'Where will you be?'

'I'm delivering a chest of drawers to Darlington.'

'OK,' I say. But it doesn't feel OK. Not one bit.

Chapter 25

In the morning, Dad's already gone by the time Eden and I eat breakfast, and we eat it in silence. She locks the door and we walk down to the bus holding our blazers close to our chests as the wind whips around us.

On the bus I sit next to a random person I don't know who is listening to their iPod and staring out of the window, and I stare past them at the blustery countryside.

The edge of Sowerbridge spreads around us and the bus stops by the school gates a few minutes later than usual.

Jodie appears from nowhere, just to ignore me, and I walk looking straight ahead into the main corridor, trying to time my pace so that I will get in in time to get a seat, but won't have to hang out in there a moment longer than necessary. There are whispers, titters, but I manage to spend five minutes finding my pencil case before tutor time kicks off. It goes OK, and I'm feeling slightly stronger, but science knocks me back. For some reason everyone gets into the chemistry block faster than me so when I go in there's nowhere to sit. I move really slowly, hoping that an opening will appear at one of the benches, but the only person to make eye contact is Oscar.

He waves.

He's so desperately desperate.

But in the end I sit with him. There's no one else.

I blunder through science, taking sidelong glances at the other girls, who are taking sidelong glances at me, while Oscar rabbits on, adding the ingredients in the wrong order so that our experiment fails and ends up looking like a glass of sick.

As the glass of chemical sick cools on the side, he melts a plastic Thermos flask and we both get sent out of the class.

I go into lunch with him. We're early, there's no one else from our year and I vaguely hope we might manage to get through it before the others come out of science. We both eat cheeseless macaroni cheese and I can see that I've become his new best friend but I feel guilty because I know I'm only using him. I suspect he knows it too.

Then quite suddenly he stands up. 'Been nice

hanging with you, Amy, but I got stuff to do, people to see,' He taps the side of his nose. 'Engineering club,' he says, and vanishes, abandoning me to a huge empty table covered in lunch rubbish and my half-eaten plate of food.

I stuff the last mouthful of macaroni in my mouth, wash it down with warm tap water and race out of the dining room, as if I had a really important appointment. Which I do, with the dead zone between the music room and the language block, which I'm hoping no one else will visit. I kill fifteen minutes leaning against the wall, checking my phone, spying on the main courtyard.

I watch Mr Zamani scraping glue from the banisters. A sixth former comes over to help him and the moment they finish, Cameron Fullick squeezes more onto the banister, much to the amusement of his group of friends.

A fight breaks out over a hat.

Someone is spectacularly macaroni cheese sick over the extractor from the science lab.

I text Isobel. *Where are you?*

My phone buzzes. Grabbing it I expect Isobel, but it's not, it's the nurse, Louise from the hospital. *Tonight. Baby Amy's new family are bringing her back to the hospital for us all to see her – would you like to come?*

This evening. But Dad's in Darlington and I can't get back from the hospital even if I could get there from school.

Oh no. I'm going to miss her.

Unless I ask Zelda.

But I can't ask Zelda.

I go into English still thinking about it. If I was talking to Jodie, I'd ask her to come with me, maybe even get her mum to give us a lift. Or Isobel, if I could get hold of her.

I look across at Oscar.

No.

I suppose I could ask Eden. But she doesn't drive.

I lay my head on my desk and let the tears flow, ignoring the giggles and pointing fingers, letting the crying come between me and the world.

Mrs Burns, the pastoral care woman, gives me a cup of tea and a box of tissues and I let the whole thing come out. Even Zelda's baby.

'Don't worry,' says Mrs Burns, pulling the door blind down. 'It's all in confidence.'

So I splurt, and blurt and rail and rant and get through the entire box of tissues and Mrs Burns looks faintly like she's been slapped around the face but she stays with me, asking a few questions, nodding, looking wise.

'So you've been helping your granny find out about this child?' she asks.

'Well, I didn't know then. I didn't know it was hers, I thought it was someone else's. I thought it was a bit of local history, but now it turns out that it's Zelda's and I have – I've been helping her . . .' The tears come in another wave.

'Yes, I see that, but did you find out anything?'

I shake my head. 'Almost nothing. It was in the hospital for a while and then fostered to some people. There's a photo at the hospital – the same hospital that Amy's in right now.' I wipe a trail of snot from my face and blow my nose again.

'Oh,' she says.

There's a sniff-filled quiet where I nearly manage to pull myself together.

'I might be able to help. Before I worked here, I was a social worker. I can tell you who to contact.'

I stare up at her. 'So you'll know what'll happen to baby Amy.'

'Yes and no.' She nods and shakes her head. 'I do. Sort of, although not exactly because every case is different. Also, things have changed since I stopped working. In the past, if she'd been fostered, she'd possibly be adopted by the same people, but it's always been a slow old process, up to about two years.'

'Will I be allowed to see her?'

'That I don't know. But now, because everyone is encouraged to talk about adoption, you will be part of her history. She'll be told about you, and Eden, and how she was found. So if she wants to see you, she'll be able to find you.'

Picking at a scrap of Sellotape on the table I imagine baby Amy as that adult again. Visiting the village, coming to stay with us. Clutching her grubby pink Babygro, the only connection with her mum.

'She's at the hospital this evening.'

'Oh?'

'But I can't get to see her – because Dad's in Darlington, and I won't ask Zelda.' I look at her hopefully. Trying to pull an endearing smile through my puffy red face.

'And I can't take you because that would be frowned upon – ask your granny. Build bridges. See if you can't forgive her. That might make you feel better about everyone else.'

'Nothing's going to make me feel better about everyone else.'

She stands, opening the door, ending my hour of sanctuary. 'See if you can. Try to see it from her point of view. Have a go, Amy.'

Chapter 26

I succeed in killing the last half-hour of the day walking corridors and I'm first onto the bus, grabbing the end of the back row. Eden comes and sits next to me with her friends and I don't think anyone else sees where I am.

'OK?' she asks.

I shake my head and she ignores me, but for her hand-holding mine, out of sight.

We get back to the village and I'm grateful to get off the bus. We link arms and wander slowly up the hill, past the bus shelter, the village hall, the empty shop and the Green Man. Les–the-sheep makes an unintelligible greeting as we alleysqueeze past him and we head on up to our house.

Eden unlocks the door and we blow in, throwing our things on the floor and sinking into chairs.

'How was it?' she asks at last.

'Awful,' I say. 'I had to spend lunch with Oscar King.'

'Eeew!' says Eden. 'Tim-who-never-washes's younger brother?'

I nod.

'Eeew again,' she says and pauses. 'But I meant, how was today with Zelda's news going round your head?

I lean over to take off my shoes. When I do, a really bad smell is going to fill the kitchen and Eden will hate me, which is more normal than Eden doing heart to heart. Eden and I never talk heart to heart, not really. We compare notes but not our souls.

'OK.'

'Because I wondered if it hurt you so much because of Mum.' She plaits the ends of a tassel hanging from her bag, and addresses the wall. This is not a moment for eye contact.

'What do you mean?

'Because we were abandoned. By Mum. She went off and left us.'

'Yes – but with Dad. That's not really a park bench or a phone box.'

'No – but it's like abandonment.'

'Hmm,' I say and go upstairs with my stinking feet.

I sit on my bed and try to work out if I do feel abandoned. Don't you have to know what you've lost to be abandoned? I mean, I didn't really know Mum when she went off with Alex to Australia. And I don't know if you can really lose a thing you never knew you had. Baby Amy barely met her mother. Zelda's baby barely met Zelda – she wouldn't know she was left behind because she'd never really clung to anyone. I had Eden and Dad, they were the solid things in my life. But the word – 'abandoned' – it's as if it means more to the abandoner than the abandonee. Amy's mum will remember more of Amy than the other way around. Zelda will remember more of her baby than her baby can possibly remember of her. And I remember almost nothing of Mum except bad temper and burnt toast. I wonder how much she thinks of us. I wonder if she thought she was running from us, or to something else.

Did we leave holes in each other's lives?

But we're not the same as those babies. There was no physical risk. We still live in the house we were born in. But Dad must remember a different time, a happier time. Eden, too.

I put on sandals and flip-flop downstairs. Yellow evening sunlight fills the garden and I open the front door so that I can sit outside. Eden joins me.

'Do you remember when she left?' she asks me.

I shake my head.

'It was weird,' she says, staring straight ahead. 'Dad was all over the place, but Zelda came and looked after us. She cooked, she read stories. She did it all so that we didn't feel deserted. There was no gap – Mum left, Zelda came in. Dad went on working. We went on playing and eating and sleeping.'

'Did she stay here?'

'Yup – with her dog, the one before Davey. He was less dogly, more houndy.'

A faint image of a dog's black gum comes into my mind.

'A yellow dog?'

'A golden thing, yes – Labrador or retriever or something.'

'And she made food?'

'All the food – we ate a lot of roast dinners and chicken soup. You don't remember?'

'No. How did Mum go? I definitely don't remember that bit.'

'She left when we were at Zelda's, and Dad was delivering something. We came back to the house in the evening. It was as if we'd been robbed. I think Dad thought we had been robbed, except the thief had

197

stolen the cookery books and the CDs and all of Mum's clothes.'

'Was it really shocking?'

Eden nods. She rubs her nose with the back of her hand. 'Zelda rescued us. All three of us. We owe her a lot.'

'So are you telling me to rush back to her with open arms?'

'I think you owe her some understanding. Some listening – some patience.' Eden gets up and goes inside. I sit staring at the light moving across the garden, lighting up different splashes of the grass, the flowers.

'Eden,' I say. 'Amy's at the hospital this evening.'

'Oh?' Eden puts her head back around the doorway.

'Yes,' I say, waiting for her to say something else. She doesn't.

'I'd love to go,' I say.

'Well, you could – you could ask Zelda.'

It's my turn not to reply.

'Does it really mean that much to you – seeing Amy?'

I nod. I daren't speak because I can feel that the floodgates are opening again.

'In that case . . .' Eden gets up and goes inside. I follow her.

'Don't ring Zelda,' I say.

'I won't,' she says. 'I'm going to call a taxi.'

We change our clothes, raid all the change piles around the house and the taxi arrives outside.

'They said twelve pounds on the phone,' says Eden, climbing in.

'That's right,' says the driver, and he pulls away from the kerb and the taxi drops gently through the village.

'Thanks, Eden,' I say.

'Well, it would be nice to see her, and I understand about Zelda – although you're going to have to come round or life's going to be really difficult.'

'Hmmm,' I say, staring out of the window.

The taxi bounces through the edge of town, whizzing us to the hospital in far less than twelve pound's worth of time.

Eden pays him as if she'd done it a million times and we find ourselves on the hospital forecourt twenty minutes after we'd thought of coming, standing too close to each other and avoiding busy-looking people with wheelchairs and clipboards.

We follow the now familiar corridors up through

the hospital to the maternity department, but it feels odd without either Dad or Zelda.

When we get to the buzzer, I hesitate.

'Go on,' says Eden.

'I'm nervous,' I say.

'I don't know why,' she says, and presses it.

'Hello?' says a voice.

'Eden and Amy to see little Amy if possible?' says Eden, sounding about twenty-five.

'Oh!' The door clicks and we push through, finding our way to the desk.

Louise, the nurse we saw in the first place is there, but she's not radiating smiles; she looks embarrassed. 'Girls!' she says. 'I didn't know you were coming.'

Eden looks at me.

'Sorry,' I stammer. 'Nor did we, it was a bit of a rush – is Amy here?'

Louise glances to the side as if the telephone might supply her with an answer. 'I'm so sorry – she came at five. We had a cup of tea, she was lovely . . .'

'Will she be back?' I ask.

Louise grimaces. 'I'm really sorry, Amy, Eden. She's not coming back anytime soon. I nearly rang you when she was here, but it was so quick and I thought you'd ring if you were coming.'

'How was she?' I hear Eden say.

'She was super, doing so well.' Louise scrumples up her nose. 'Like a proper baby in a proper family. But I'm so sorry you missed her.'

'I totally understand,' I say. 'Totally – that's fine, thanks – we – totally . . .' I turn as fast as I can and head out of the department, pressing the button that opens the door from the inside and getting out into the corridor as fast as I can without actually running. Eden bundles along behind me and we stop, leaning against the wall, under a giant yellow vinyl octopus.

Neither of us speaks. I feel stupid for not checking, for assuming, for failing to ring. I'm guessing Eden's feeling stupid for believing me.

After a couple of minutes I push away from the wall and head down towards the main foyer. Eden follows. Still silent.

We stand next to each other on the pavement outside the hospital breathing hard, swallowing, keeping it together.

'Let's get a cup of tea,' she says in the end. 'And a KitKat.'

'Can we afford it?' I say.

'Yup – I think so. We only need twelve pounds to get back again.' So I follow her into the Friends Cafe

201

and we drink overly strong tea from thick blue china cups and share a Twix.

We still don't talk. I'm not sure I'd know what to say, but in the end I just say, 'Sorry. I should have rung.'

She shrugs. 'So should I.'

I sigh.

She sighs.

She picks up her phone. 'Seven-thirty,' she says. 'I'll call a taxi.'

I read a notice board while she makes the call.

'Sixteen?' she says. 'But it was only twelve to get here.'

'Really?' she says.

'No – no, not now – I'll call you back.' She closes her phone case and stares briefly at the floor.

'What did they say?' I ask.

'They said it would be sixteen pounds to take us home.'

'Sixteen? Why?'

'Because it's after seven and their rates go up in the evenings.'

'But that's . . .'

'Extortion,' she says. 'I know.'

'We could check the bus?' I say, pointing at the bus at the end of the car park.

It turns out that there's one in half an hour that would take us to the centre of town. 'But then we'd have to take another one to get home and I don't think there is one after eight and we might not make it,' says Eden, looking very tired.

'We're going to have to ring Zelda, aren't we?' I say, wondering if today can actually get any worse.

Eden twists her mouth to the side in doubt. 'Well, yes,' she says. 'I don't think there's any choice.'

Zelda doesn't try to make conversation. She doesn't do any more than pick us up and drop us off. She isn't cross, she isn't pleased to see us. In fact, she behaves like a taxi driver, all except for the money. It leaves me feeling really guilty.

'Thank you,' says Eden, giving her a kiss goodbye.

I hesitate between the door and the car, aware of a stupid half-smile on my face and I flap my hand at Zelda in what I hope seems like a tired thank-you.

She swoops off, the red lights on the Mini lighting up the stone wall opposite, and we go into the house.

'Do you want anything to eat?' asks Eden. 'I could cook some pasta.'

But I don't. All I want is my bed and the darkness and a large hole in which to hide myself.

Chapter 27

'Amy!' yells Isobel across the courtyard a second after I arrive at school. She runs towards me, beaming, and throws her arm and her shoulder bag around me. 'Ace,' she says. 'You're here.'

'Isobel,' I say and try really hard not to cry with relief. 'Where have you been?'

'Broke my arm, didn't I?' She holds up her wrist. There's a heavy white cast jammed inside her blazer sleeve. 'Had to spend the night in hospital while they reset it and then like days and days without being able to text.'

'How?'

'As I got home, I tripped and cracked it on the doorstep.' She face palms. 'Stupid me.'

'I'm so glad you're here,' I say. 'It's all gone a bit . . .' I make a face to try to approach the horror of the last few days.

'Jodie?' she says.

I nod.

'You didn't accuse her – did you?' Her eyes and mouth grow wide as she realises that I did. 'You idiot, Amy – you can't do this, you've got to be more . . . well, less, obvious.'

'I know – now,' I say.

She links her arm in mine and sweeps me through the middle of a large group of Year Nines, who mutter and try faintly to stand their ground but give way in the face of Isobel's cheerfulness.

'So do you think you need to apologise to her? Or her to you?'

'She needs to apologise to me,' I say firmly. 'I think.'

'But that's assuming she stole your purse.'

'But she did. Didn't she? I mean, who else did?'

'Oh, for goodness' sake,' she says, pulling me round to face her. 'It was so long ago – does it matter? Just apologise, clear the air, break the habit of a lifetime and let it go. Anyway – we're going to be late for tutor time – c'mon.'

'Zelda's asked if you would come round,' says Dad when I get home.

He and Eden stare at me. 'No,' I say, in the end, *Just apologise, clear the air, break the habit of a lifetime*, ringing in my head as I do. 'I can't.'

'She wants to go on the dodgems, the fair's on in Sowerbridge, and she thought you might go with her.'

'Oh,' I say, picking up my bag and thumping up the stairs to my room.

'Think about it,' Dad calls.

I do. I sit on my bed and I think about it, and in the end I decide that the dodgems would be all right, but only if Dad and Eden come too, to stop me strangling Zelda.

Miraculously, when I come downstairs, Zelda's already there, waiting, perfect in neat black trousers and flat shoes, as if she'd known I was going to cave in.

Dad drives and Eden and I sit silently in the back eating either end of a baguette. Dad puts the radio on and we listen to fragments of the news.

The fun fair is in a park on the edge of Sowerbridge, and Dad spends ages finding a parking space so that by the time we walk over to the fair, the sky's turning dark and the lights are more orange and more magic. The fairground music thumps through the ground beneath our feet and the mixed smells of oil and sausages float across the air. Muddy grass stretches underneath all the rides, disappearing as the darkness creeps up. And the badly painted stalls fade into obscurity as the shiny and the loud take over. Very quickly, Zelda heads towards the dodgems, and produces her purse to pay for four tokens. Dad folds himself into a black one and I choose a mean green machine, opposite Eden's red Noddy car. Zelda must be behind me because I can't see her and we all sit waiting, swinging the steering wheels, listening to the music from the other rides.

Without warning, the dodgems spring into life. 'Ticket to Ride' blares out over the exhausted sound system and my car leaps into motion, lurching backwards at speed. I swing the wheel round and stop, jamming my foot on the pedal so that I ram the back of Dad's car.

'Amy!' he shouts, and within a second is in hot pursuit. I race away, clipping Eden's car and spinning her round before heading straight for Zelda. I see the look of horror on her face before my car ploughs into the side of hers, sending us both sideways. She's quicker than I am and avoids Dad, who charges the rear of my car and bounces off into Eden. Getting the hang of it, I get the accelerator flat on the floor and home in on Zelda, thumping her car twice and again jamming her into the parked mass of unused dodgems. I scoot off and the guy running it climbs over and releases Zelda's car so that before I've even done a circuit she's bearing down on me, her mouth open wide, screaming with laughter. I swing my car round and ram hers, both of us thumping hard. Then Dad rams me, then I ram Dad, then Eden rams me and Zelda and then we all ram each other and then the machine runs out of time and we glide to a halt and stagger to the side.

'That was great,' laughs Zelda. 'Thank you, all.'

'It was,' says Dad, leaning over and getting his breath back.

'Brilliant,' says Eden. 'Wish we could do that at school.'

'Yes,' I say, wondering where all my anger has gone. 'It was fantastic – thank you, Zelda, thank you, Dad. I really enjoyed it.'

We eat sausages and pick at a solid mass of chips on the way back. They taste of oil. Mostly chip oil, but with a hint of lorries. But we're so hungry that they're almost delicious. Zelda buys two cans, which we share and then we all sing Beatles songs, all the way home, and it's funny because not only has the anger gone, but I actually feel cheerful for the first time in days. Positive, like I can manage. I can do this.

So When Zelda asks if I can help her find Deidre, the baby from all those years ago, I can't think why I wouldn't.

'Yes, of course,' I say. 'I'll come over on Saturday.'

Chapter 28

On Saturday we start again. We really do. We start by giving each other a hug and she says, 'Sorry, darling,' and I say, 'Sorry, Zelda.' And then we hug again.

It feels a bit weird but really, it's definitely the right thing to do. Eden was right.

I sit at her counter-top and drink hot chocolate with marshmallows and she lets me make a teapot full of sweet iced tea for later.

She shows me a letter from Pamela, big, loopy, messy handwriting inviting herself to stay.

'Brilliant!' I say. 'So she's coming to stay.'

We write down everything we know. And everything we don't. Which is bigger.

We have no idea what happened after that photo.

We don't know if there was an adoption agency or if it was done privately, We don't know if she was adopted by the same people who fostered her.

We don't know where the couple lived.

We don't know anything very much.

'So you left her in the church porch on Midsummer Day,' I say. 'What do you remember?'

'I remember the birth, in the barn – Pamela's barn. It was – anyway, it was birth, and luckily it went all right.'

'Did you give her a name?'

'I called her Eve.'

'Let's call her Eve, then – it's better than Deidre.'

'And we dressed Eve – I had bought some little boot things and a pair of pyjamas from a jumble sale. And there was a knitted cardi from when I was a baby – I took that, along with terry nappies that my mother had kept and used for making jam.'

'Oh!'

Zelda smiles. 'They were slightly purple, I remember wrapping them around that tiny bottom. We hadn't a clue what we were doing, of course, and she was so small. Pamela washed her, boiling water and lugging it down the farm yard. I even tried feeding her, but again I'd no idea what I was doing and Pamela produced a bottle of special milk for babies so we tried to give her that. It was a lovely afternoon and we sat in the straw and ran through all the possibilities. In the end, we felt it best to find somewhere to leave her, somewhere she'd be found. Pamela suggested

211

the pub toilets but I was worried some drunk person would fall over her. Then we thought about the school, but I worried no one would find her for days. I think it was a Saturday.

'School?'

'There used to be one in the village – Martin went to it. I even wondered about leaving her on our own doorstep – or Pamela's but then the secret would come out, bound to.' Zelda draws a circle on the paper. 'So the church seemed the best answer. There was going to be a midsummer service at ten o'clock so I knew she'd be found before nightfall – also there was a metal screen in the door that meant the birds couldn't get in. I knew there'd be no dogs or cats or anything.'

'So you walked to the church?'

'We took her on our bikes.'

'You rode a bike after giving birth?'

'It wasn't easy, but it's tougher in other parts of the world. Farming women in some countries give birth in the fields and then go back to work. It's possible – not ideal, but possible. Eve was so small she fitted in the bike basket on the front. She was good as gold, not a sound.' Zelda stops and gazes up towards the ceiling. I let her stop and think, and after a moment she seems to wake up again. 'Anyway, we left our bikes by the field gate, the one no one uses. The cow parsley was high and we waded through it, Pamela carrying Eve. I couldn't do it. She was asleep and we left her in the porch, in the collecting bowl. You know? The big wooden one they hand around at Christmas.'

'Gosh,' I say.

We both sit, thinking.

'I kissed her and left her. I'm not sure if I even cried – I think it was all too traumatic.'

Zelda's looking into the past – I don't think she's even aware she's sitting in her kitchen in the twenty-first century.

'And your parents never knew?'

She shakes her head. 'Dad was so conventional, it would have destroyed him, and Mum always did what he said, although I think I could have told her – but I never did.'

She gets up and fills the kettle.

'What was in the jam jar? The one I found when we were looking for raspberry jam.'

'The jam jar,' she repeats, 'Oh! I'll show you.'

She reaches into the cupboard with the coffee and the tea and brings down the jar. She unscrews the lid and pulls out a square of fabric. A dark blue summer print with little red cherries.

'It used to be a skirt,' she says. 'See, here?' She flattens the fabric on the table.

'There's a little chunk missing,' I say.

'Yes, it was about a square inch. I thought I could cut it out of the hem and my mother wouldn't notice. I put it with her – wrapped up in the pocket of the matinee jacket. I needed to give her something and I didn't have anything. It was the only thing I could think of.'

Zelda strokes the cloth, flattening the ancient creases.

'It was my broken token. She had some, I had some, in case . . .' She strokes it against her cheek and lets out a huge sob that shakes her shoulders.

I sit staring at the pepper pot, rethinking everything I ever thought.

Chapter 29

At school it's all about Jodie. I've tried to clear the air with her, I really have, but she won't talk.

She's hanging out with a bunch of girls I've never got on with. 'Oh, Amy,' she says, sticking her nose in the air and sailing past me. 'She used to be a friend.'

'Jodie,' I say to her back. 'Sorry – OK?'

But she won't turn, and she won't listen, so I let it slide.

And the whispering keeps going, but on the whole it doesn't bother me. I don't hear it, and it can't touch me. My mind's on other things now. It's like it's become Jodie's problem – if she won't let me apologise, then what more can I do?

At break Isobel finds me and I tell her that I want to see Mrs Burns.

'Why?'

We go to the dead space by the music room and I tell her about Zelda, Pamela and the baby.

She's silent for a long time and then she says, 'Poor

things, poor all of them. Thank you for telling me. But why Mrs Burns?'

'She used to be a social worker – she knows how this stuff works.' Mrs Burns is invisible at break so we have to go through textiles before we can find her, which means we get to see Miss Brownell explode when Oscar sews himself to his Minecraft pencil case.

In Spanish I sense Jodie's eyes staring at the back of my neck, but I hold my head higher and ignore her and Isobel meets me at lunch to go and find Mrs Burns. We have to wait – she's dealing with a scrap between Year Sevens and I only have a second to talk before the bell rings.

'Amy, how are you? You look better. You're obviously getting on with Isobel, that's nice to see.'

'And Granny Zelda,' I say. 'It's just Jodie now. I keep trying, but . . .' I shrug.

'It'll sort itself out in the end,' she says, not looking a bit like she believes it.

'You know you used to be a social worker?' I say. 'Would I be able to talk to you about the finding out stuff?'

Mrs Burns looks at her watch. 'Well, I've a meeting now, and you should be in classes, but I could see you at 3.15.'

'Brilliant,' I say. 'See you then.'

I barely notice biology. I certainly don't notice Jodie standing there with a doleful expression and I only just remember to tell Eden that I'm not coming home on the bus.

'How are you going to get back?' she says, running towards the bus stop.

'Dunno,' I say. 'I'll work it out.'

Mrs Burns is late, so I wonder if she's forgotten but when she comes back to her office she's got a stack of print-outs with her.

'Sorry for being late, Amy – but I rang up a friend who's up to date and she sent through these. They're just the procedure for contacting someone who has been adopted.'

'Do you mean Zelda can find out what happened to her baby? Just like that?'

Mrs Burns shakes her head. 'It's not as simple as that – it's possible that if she lodges a request with an Adoption Support Agency, and if they can access the general register of adoptions – then they can contact your grandmother's daughter and see if she wishes to make contact.'

'Great!'

'But, Amy, there are things that might get in the

way. One, it was before 1975, so there was less regulation, which makes it harder – she might not have been adopted in the ordinary way. The second is, she may not want to make contact. She may feel it would be too hard for her to meet the woman who . . .'

'Rejected her?'

'I didn't want to say that, but yes.'

I watch someone do a really bad cartwheel outside the window.

'We'll have to see, won't we. But thank you. Thank you so much. At least we know where to start.'

Zelda's waiting outside in the Mini.

'And?' she says.

I explain about Adoption Support Agencies and about 1975 and about the fact that the now-fifty-year-old woman might not want to make contact.

'I see,' says Zelda, and she rolls down the window, letting the warmth of early May rush past us. 'I see.'

We race out of the town and through the lanes, dandelions and buttercups bouncing their heads as we whizz past. She stops, by the church.

'I haven't been in, you know,' she says. 'Not since that day.'

And I realise I've never seen her in the church. That

218

we go to the carol service and she doesn't – always meeting us up at the pub afterwards.

'Do you want to?' I ask.

'Come on – it's silly – I should.'

We get out of the car. Les-the-sheep and Beau wander past, and he nods at me, nods at Zelda and shoots us a look as if he's working something out.

'Does he know?' I ask, Zelda.

'Pretty sure he does – he'll have put two and two together. He was an observant lad, even then, and we'd have been noisy, coming up to the church. Our bikes were leaning against the wall and we were sitting just there – beyond the compost bins. But, bless him, he's never said a word about it.'

We push open the lych gate and wander up the path between the ancient gravestones, some yawning, some almost submerged. The outer gate is open. I pull it and we stand in the porch, blinking at the dark.

'Here,' she says. 'Here's where I left her.' She points at the bench to the right of the door.

I don't know what to say. So I nod, sagely, and hope that it's doing whatever it needs to do for Zelda.

'Right,' she shrugs. 'I'll drop you at home – school tomorrow.'

Chapter 30

On Friday night, Pamela comes to stay with Zelda and we go to meet her train. The four of us, and Dad takes us all to the pub in Midhinton on the way home. It's a warm evening so we sit outside with Coke and crisps and our ankles get savaged by midges and licked by Davey. Pamela's almost the opposite of Zelda. Big and cushiony and comforting, with a rattly smoker's laugh and sagging everything. I can see that she makes Zelda feel safe, and probably has done ever since their childhood.

'So which is which?' she asks, looking from me to Eden.

'Eden,' says Eden. 'I'm the one in the middle of exams.'

'And I'm Amy,' I say, suddenly feeling self-conscious.

'Aren't you both lovely,' says Pamela, her face stretched wide with a smile. 'Just lovely.'

She and Dad and Zelda chat about the village, the

pub, the people Pamela remembers, the people Pamela's forgotten.

'What about that boy that used to hang about all the time? What happened to him?'

'Les?' asks Zelda.

'Was that his name? I don't remember, I just remember he was always around, always there whenever you turned round. Watching.' She shudders.

'Still is,' says Dad.

I think about Les-the-sheep. It's true, he is always there, always watching.

'I always thought it was a bit creepy,' says Pamela.

'No!' I exclaim. 'I think of him as keeping an eye on everything.'

'Which he does, of course,' says Dad. 'He stopped us all flooding a year or so back because he spotted a blocked drain in Picketts Lane.'

'And he found Mr Carson lying in his hallway after the heart attack,' says Zelda.

Everyone nods while we think about Les, but no one actually says what we're all thinking.

Until Pamela does. 'It was him, wasn't it?'

'At the church?' says Zelda. 'Yes, he found her.' Zelda looks at us. 'I told Pamela that you knew about it. The church, the porch, Eve – all of it.'

Pamela takes a sip from her glass of wine. 'So what do you all think about Margaret's baby?'

Eden looks completely blank, and I'm sure I do too.

'You have to call me "Zelda", dear,' says Zelda. 'They don't know who Margaret is.' She shifts on the bench and traces the grain of the wood with her fingernail.

'It came as a bit of a shock,' says Dad. 'To be honest, I'm still brought up short by the idea I have a half-sister out there somewhere.' But he smiles at Zelda, and there's no anger in his voice.

Pamela nods. 'And you, girls?'

Eden says, 'I think it's kind of exciting, my friends think it's quite exciting. Not that Zelda had a baby when she was my age, that must have been scary, but that we've got another relation out there – but I know Amy had a bit of a struggle with the thought – didn't you?'

I nod. I don't want to say too much or get angry when on the whole I don't feel angry any more, so it's better that I don't say anything at all. I quickly examine my feelings about what I think and I find that I don't really feel anything now but curiosity.

'I do hope you haven't told all your friends,' says Zelda. 'I wouldn't want everyone to know – I don't feel very good about it . . . . I don't think I want it to be public knowledge.'

'Only my really close ones,' says Eden, reddening, and I wonder if everyone in Year Eleven knows. The only one of my friends who knows is Isobel, and I trust her completely.

Now.

'So have you got anywhere with trying to find her?' asks Pamela.

Zelda coughs on her drink and looks around to check there's no one nearby. 'Yes and no,' she says. 'Sort of. I've made contact with an agency who are looking – but of course I've no evidence, no means of her identifying me. Apart from the date and place, which someone could fake. Do you remember that little scrap of fabric, from my skirt? Well, if that scrap of fabric . . .' Zelda swallows, and takes a moment to readjust her glasses. 'If that fabric hasn't survived – and there's no mention of it in Sergeant Godwin's account – then I can't identify her at all. She wouldn't know if I was really . . .' Her voice cracks at the end, but she does a good job of covering it by leaning over to fondle Davey's disgusting ears.

Dad sighs. 'So you wouldn't even know her if you saw her and she wouldn't know you.'

'There's that tiny photo,' I say. 'Although it's black and white and very small.'

'How frustrating,' says Pamela. 'I thought these things were much more straightforward.'

'What about DNA tests?' says Eden.

'Oh, if it comes to those, then obviously it's a question of a match, but in the first instance we need more things that connect her with me. Even if they let us, we couldn't DNA test everyone who was adopted in 1966. It could take years.'

'There was the birthmark,' says Pamela.

'I don't remember that,' says Zelda.

'In her hair – she had a large strawberry mark. I suppose it was on the back of her head. I remember it, partly because it wouldn't wash off when I bathed her in that bucket in the barn, but also because it was in the shape of an apple.'

'How marvellous – they'd know we really – I really was her mother. If I knew that.' Zelda laughs almost happily. 'Is that why we called her Eve?'

'Probably,' says Pamela. 'It's so long ago.'

Both women stare into the middle distance, looking into their memories.

Chapter 31

I don't hear anything from Zelda for a week or two. She doesn't drop round. She doesn't invite herself for tea. I find I have my own problems though.

'There's a bad smell in here,' says Jodie, in a tone that stings. 'Oh – Amy's here, that's why.'

She sails past me and sits on the other side of the classroom. I keep looking straight ahead and avoid any eye contact with anyone else.

We're in maths, which means there's no one to hide behind. Oscar's too clever to be in my maths group and Isobel's at a singing lesson so I'm going to have to weather it on my own.

I pretend not to notice her and fiddle around with my pencil case.

'Who else are we waiting for?' asks someone.

'There's Amy, over there,' says Jodie. 'She's a tad, you know – abandoned.'

Mrs Simonez comes in and fiddles with the laptop connected to the overhead projector.

We settle down. Something hits me on the back.

By the sound it makes when it hits the floor, it's a pencil.

Bump

Another pencil.

And another.

It doesn't really hurt, but it's making me jumpy. It's not like this stuff hasn't been happening for months – but not quite like this.

I lean down to pick up one of the pencils and another clips me on the top of my ear.

I sit up and one scoots across my desk and lands by Mrs Simonez. She turns round and looks at me.

'Amy?' she questions.

'It's not me,' I say. 'It's someone else.'

Mrs Simonez raises her eyebrows and goes back to fixing the projector.

I get my phone out to check the time and a chorus goes up behind me. 'Miss, she's got her phone out – Miss, she's ringing someone.'

'I'm not,' I say to the air.

'Miss, she's going to make a phone call.'

Mrs Simonez sighs and turns on the projector, which sends a square of light across the classroom onto the wall.

I try to concentrate on the words on the screen but another pencil wings across the classroom and thwacks into my cheek.

I can't help it.

It bubbles up and I simply can't stop it.

'Jodie!' I yell and stand up, facing her, my back to the screen. 'What the hell is wrong with you?'

'What?' says Jodie. 'I didn't do anything, although I know you think I'm a thief.'

'I don't,' I say. 'I don't think anyone's a thief. I've tried to apologise a million times. '

'Girls,' says Mrs Simonez. 'This is not the time nor the place – would you put your differences away.'

But Jodie's got no intention of doing that and she comes round the desk so that we're facing each other and there's nothing in between.

'Girls . . .' starts Mrs Simonez.

'She thinks everyone's stolen stuff from her – thinks one of us stole her stupid purse. She's accusing us one after the other because of course she's completely perfect.'

'What?' I say.

'But she isn't because her family holds a deep and cruel secret!'

I should turn and leave.

'It turns out that perfect Amy has a less than perfect granny.'

A titter runs through the room.

'Jodie,' warns Mrs Simonez. 'Be careful.'

'That her lovely, smiley granny did a dreadful crime when she was just a teenager.'

'Jodie,' I say. 'Please don't.'

'She had a baby . . .'

The room falls pindrop silent.

'. . . And she abandoned it.'

There's a gasp.

'On its little bitty own in the church in the cold where it might have died – and she walked away and left it. So how lovely is she now? How lovely are they? Anyone see a hypocrite here?' She looks around theatrically.

I should definitely leave at this point.

But I don't.

Mrs Burns isn't quite as sympathetic this time around. Not least because I caught a chunk of Jodie's hair in my bag strap when I tried to strangle her.

Well, I didn't really try to strangle her, but I was angry enough to make her think I would.

I spend the afternoon apologising and writing a

letter to Jodie's mum to explain why Jodie's shirt is all torn before Mrs Burns finally relents and asks me why I went for her.

'Because she told everyone about Zelda, my grandma, and her baby.'

'Oh!' Mrs Burns sits down.

I draw an elephant on the blank pad of paper in front of me.

'But how did she know?' I ask.

Mrs Burns sits back and purses her lips. 'So who have you told – apart from me? Isobel?'

I draw another elephant.

'I did tell Isobel, but I trust her. I'm sure she wouldn't say anything to anyone.'

'Who else knows?

'My Dad, Eden . . .' and I remember Eden talking about her friends.

Mrs Burns watches me as I work out what I'm thinking. 'Eden's best friend is in a drama club with Jodie.'

'Oh dear,' she says.

Rats.

'So how are you going to build a bridge with Jodie? You can't go on tearing her hair out all year, you know – the headmaster won't like it.'

Chapter 32

We go away for two nights to Cornwall over half-term. Dad's got this huge piece of furniture to deliver, so he's hired a van and Eden and I are getting to go along for the ride. Before we do, Dad decides that we need to empty the laundry basket.

'You mean wash every last little bit at the bottom? Even Amy's reindeer slippers?' Eden recoils.

'Every horrible little thing – it's lovely drying weather – those foul slippers can hang on the line while we're away. I don't even know if they're washable – but I can't stand the idea of them lurking down there any longer.'

My furry reindeer slippers have been in there since Christmas – infusing everything that goes in the laundry basket with a smell that's similar to Davey's. They were a present from Aunty May, but they got wet and the leather started to stink. Dad said to bung them in the laundry basket, so I did, but they never got washed. They might actually be made of reindeer.

Dad drags the basket outside and we ritually turn it upside down.

He bashes the bottom and there's a flump as everything hits the grass.

Removing the basket we rush forward to examine the pile of crunkled remnants. The reindeer slippers are the largest items. I lift one with a stick.

'Ha!' Dad stands back, laughing. 'They're not that bad!'

'They are!' says Eden, running away as I poke it in her direction. 'Stop it!' I wave the slipper and chase her round the garden through the apple trees until we're both hysterical with laughter. Behind us Dad leans down and picks the last few items out of the pile.

'Three odd socks and, what's this?' he stands. 'Amy?'

Slowing, I drop the stick and turn round.

Dad's holding something up. Something furry. Something that looks kind of like the reindeer slippers, but actually more like a kangaroo.

'Amy! No! Your purse!' yells Eden across the garden.

I feel the blush race up my chest. 'My purse?' I whisper. 'Oh no.' And I remember that night, the night we found baby Amy, emptying my PE kit into the laundry basket. I just opened my bag and dropped everything in.

Without looking.

'I never checked it properly.'

'Oh, Amy,' says Dad.

In Cornwall, we stay in a boat in a harbour. It's cosy, cut off and we play cards and chat while Eden worries about her exams and Dad says exams don't matter. Not really, not in the scheme of things. On the second night we eat a reheated cauliflower cheese that Dad brought with us all the way from home and when the rain stops we sit on the deck and enjoy the sun and the slight smell of old fish.

We stay up there on the deck until the darkness sets in and the sky goes from green to black.

Over Monopoly we discuss baby Amy and Zelda. 'Are you still angry with Zelda and baby Amy's mum?' asks Eden, buying Old Kent Road.

'No,' I say. 'I almost understand it now. They kind of had no choice. Zelda didn't – and who knows about baby Amy's mum – she was probably desperate. I'm just sad about them. Ooh! A Get out of Jail Free card. That makes two.'

'What about the purse – have you told Isobel? Jodie?' says Dad.

I shake my head.

He leaves it, but Eden's less kind.

'What an idiot,' says Eden.

'You're an idiot for telling Madeleine Perez about Zelda's baby – she must have told Jodie.'

Something that I recognise as a blush creeps slowly across Eden's face. 'Oh no – is that where . . . ? I hardly even said anything. I never . . .'

'Oh dear,' says Dad, and then he says, 'We all make mistakes.'

'Sorry about that,' says Eden. 'But you're a bigger idiot.'

'Yes,' I say, letting her words fall on me without having an argument.

'I mean, why didn't you check your PE kit at home? It's cringeworthy.'

'Eden,' warns Dad.

'Why didn't you keep your big mouth shut?' I snap, feeling the anger rise and then slide away.

'Girls,' says Dad, in a serious, almost cross kind of a way. 'As I said, we all make mistakes. The thing is to learn from them, understand why we made them, repair them when we can, and move on.'

I breathe in and out, slowly. 'I was wrong. I was angry with Isobel for not inviting me to her sleep-over – and I was angry with everything that happened afterwards. I wanted something to blame her for. The purse was . . .' I shrug. 'And actually going around accusing people, was . . .' I feel a hot burst of tears welling up behind my eyes and blink furiously. '. . . stupid.'

Eden puts her arm around me and squeezes me in a hug, which makes the tears spill over and pour down my face.

Dad looks over at us and his own eyes become watery, and he sniffs, frantically fighting it. 'Oh dear,' he says. 'I suppose if you'd been less sure you might have looked for it in the laundry basket.'

I nod, pulling away from Eden, trying to swallow the tears, failing, and talking through them in a stuttery kind of a way. 'But I had no idea it would blow up like it did. I kind of expected whoever it was to come clean and give it back.' I roll the dice, wipe my sleeve across my eyes before moving my piece along the board. 'Or that it would be obvious who'd taken it – there wouldn't be all this noise and months of all these people taking offence.'

'To be fair – they have behaved like idiots too.' Eden buys Pall Mall.

'Ah but they're just people, behaving like people do – and maybe you hadn't really allowed for people behaving like people,' says Dad, with a smile, taking his turn and landing on Fenchurch St.

'No, I say. 'I hadn't – I thought they'd behave more sensibly. And you owe me £50 rent, please,' I sniff, 'because I own two stations.'

Chapter 33

On the way home Dad buys a newspaper. There's a picture of baby Amy inside. This time with her new foster parents, Erin and Mike.

'*Police are still appealing to the mother of baby Amy to come forward,*' reads Eden.

'She won't now, surely,' says Dad.

'Seems a bit late,' says Eden.

I take the paper from Eden and examine the photo – I can't tell if little Amy looks happy. If she knows she's been rescued.

'Your mum'll ring tonight. She said she'd call after supper,' says Dad.

'Oh,' I say.

'You'll be pleased to talk to her – won't you?' he says. I can't see his face as Eden's in between us. He sounds falsely jolly.

'I can tell her about my exams,' says Eden.

The dual carriageway narrows and the car slows at the end of a long line of traffic, following a tractor. I don't know what I think about Mum calling. I don't want to tell her about baby Amy again, it's not for me to talk about Zelda – and if I tell her about the stuff at school she'll be all understanding and I'll feel worse. I'll have to think of something else.

'Fine,' I say to the air. 'Fine.'

When we get home, there's a message from Zelda jammed in the door.

Have major news. Love, Zelda.

Although Dad looks completely shattered, we wander across the village to Zelda's. The windows are open, the irises are almost over and beautiful dark pink gladioli surround her cottage doorway. She's sitting on her bench and smiles at us as we walk up her path.

'How are you?' she says. 'Did you have a nice time?'

'Yes, yes, but what is it?' I ask.

She smiles. 'She wants to meet me.'

'Like that? Out of the blue?' I say.

'Yes.' Zelda's eyes are glowing with excitement. 'Apparently she's been looking for me and the adoption agency has been working hard. Pamela was right about the birthmark – we can still have a DNA test, of course, but everything else sounds very positive.'

237

'Oh, Zelda!' says Dad. 'Is this wise?'

'It's the best thing ever,' Zelda giggles.

'But you might not like her,' I say. 'She might not like you.'

Zelda purses her lips. 'I know. I know all these things, and I know it can be difficult and that even if she likes me she may not be very likeable herself – after all, we've had very different lives – but I've been worrying about this since 1966. If I don't meet her, I –' she waves her hands – 'I might just go mad.'

'What is her name?' I ask. 'Is it still Deidre?'

'No,' says Zelda. 'It's Kate now. Kate Smith. A very simple name, I thought.'

'Better than Eve Fray,' I say.

'God, that would have been her name,' says Zelda. 'I hadn't even thought about that.'

'Can we meet her?' says Eden.

'Yes,' I say, linking arms with Eden. 'Can we?'

'If she wants to. Yes. But in the first instance, I'm getting you, Martin, to come with me to London to meet her for coffee, with the woman from the adoption place. You will, won't you?'

Dad looks panicky and then says, 'Of course I will, of course.'

* * *

Something that might be butterflies sets up in my stomach. It's a good butterflies, but it stops me concentrating and I've completely forgotten Mum when the computer makes weird pinging noises and I remember that she's going to Skype us.

'Amy – honey – how are you? All brown I see, from Cornwall. How was it? And how's everybody?

'Fine,' I say, trying to think of something more but buzzing with Zelda's baby's butterflies.

'How are your friends? Jodie and Isobel – are you getting along at the moment?'

'Um . . .' I pause. 'Yeah – yes, totally great and fine.'

'Really?' she prods.

'Yeah, sure – it's all good. How are the twins?'

'They're good.'

'And Alex?'

I always ask after Alex, because it's polite and I should but I don't care about him. 'He's good, thanks, Amy. He's off to visit his mother in Melbourne this week so the twins and me are all on our ownsome.'

'Oh.'

There's a pause.

'So I hope nothing goes wrong while he's away – I'm an ignoramus when it comes to the house. You know, fixing things and all of that.'

'Gosh,' I say. 'So he's abandoning you for a while.'

'Yes!' says Mum. 'Oh and let me get the twins to show you something they did. Alice! Daisy!' Mum yells off screen and two blonde heads appear at the bottom, bounding around her knees.

'Hi, Amy! Look what I did!' they both shout.

A scribble on a piece of white paper flashes in front of the screen. I can't really make it out, but it might be a face.

'And me,' shouts the other one, flapping another piece of paper at the screen.

'Great,' I say. 'It's hard to see them from here. What are they?'

'The darlings,' says Mum, her mouth showing above the bobbing heads. 'Pictures of their daddy – Alex – aren't they marvellous?'

And Mum looks down on them, her face full of love, and I wonder if Eden's right. That all this hurts so much more because of Mum. Because she did abandon us, she left us to be rescued by Zelda, to survive alone while she turned the sun of her attention on her new family in Australia. And I wonder, as I look at her on the other side of the world, if she'll ever regret it. Like Zelda did. Whether she'll seek us out for laughs and love, and whether, when she does, we'll welcome her back.

'Bye, Mum,' I say.

'Bye, darling,' she says. 'Miss you.'

'Miss you,' I say, for probably the first time ever.

She sort of coughs, and she closes the connection.

I stare at the blank screen wondering at myself, wondering if I'd actually like to see her again, properly, face to face – and deciding that I probably would.

Chapter 34

Zelda and Dad go together to meet Kate Smith, AKA Deidre, AKA Eve, on Saturday. I go into town to hang out with Isobel because apparently she thinks we really need to buy some summer clothes together.

We're sitting in the milkshake shop at the bottom of town.

I have chosen something that Dad would describe as 'inedibily sweet'. It's a chocolate caramelly milk-shake with a Mars bar in it. Isobel has something gravelly made of Oreo biscuits and Terry's chocolate orange. Personally, I think it's a mistake.

'So what happens if they get on? Will she come and live with you? Live with your granny?'

I choke on the sweetness of my milkshake. It actually makes my eyes water. 'No – she's a woman in her fifties, she'll have her own life,' I say, quoting something that Dad said.

'Oh – I suppose so,' says Isobel. 'But won't it be extraordinary – meeting someone like that, I mean a person who has the same genes but that you don't know?'

'A long-lost aunt?'

'Oh, Jodie!' Isobel jumps up from the table and rushes out to the street, and before I've got a chance to run, drags her back into the cafe.

There's a moment when Jodie stares and I know that I must look like a rabbit in the headlights, but Isobel ignores us both and sits Jodie down at the table, offering her a straw and a go on her black, gritty milkshake.

'Hi,' says Jodie. 'I didn't know . . .'

'Nor did I,' I say.

'Exactly,' says Isobel.

I glare at Isobel, but she smiles in a way that lets me right into her thoughts, and I know she's made this happen on purpose.

It's awkward, but it works and we have a good time in the milkshake place ordering Jodie another dubious combination of cream and biscuits. Isobel takes a selfie, which we share and it makes us look like the best friends ever – rather than three people tip-toeing around each other.

I look at the other two, smiling and almost seeming relaxed, and I take a deep breath.

'Listen,' I say. 'I need to tell you something.'

'I need to say something first,' says Jodie.

'Oh,' I say.

'It's like – sorry,' she says, immediately sucking through her straw.

'Did you say "sorry"?' says Isobel.

Jodie nods her head, her hair falling around her face. 'Sorry about what I said, in school, about your gran – and the baby.'

'Oh,' I say. Amazed.

'It must have hurt,' says Jodie. 'But I was angry, and . . .'

'Yes,' I say. Wondering how to say what I need to say.

There's this long pause. Almost as long as a whole song on the radio.

'What happened about the baby you found?' asks Jodie in the end.

'She's been fostered,' I say.

'Did you find her mum?' asks Jodie.

I shake my head. 'No – and perhaps it's just as well. She's probably better off now.'

Jodie nods her head, I nod, Isobel nods. We all nod, like wise people. We're still nodding when Isobel says, 'So, what was it that you wanted to say before, Amy?

Is it exciting?' She giggles and shuffles her shoulders. She's either really embarrassed or she's imagining that I'm about to announce that I've been picked to sing on *Britain's Got Talent* or that Dad's getting married.

'The purse.'

The giggles vanish.

'Yes?' Isobel helps me.

'I found it. In the laundry bin at home. It had been there ever since we did PE on the day it went missing. The day I found baby Amy. And I'm sorry, I'm really sorry that I accused you both because I know it wasn't anything to do with you, it was . . .'

I gulp back the tears, and both of them stand, lean over the table and hold me, almost giving me a full, proper hug, but with just a little bit held back. All of us holding back, just a little bit.

We go shopping together, for the first time in months. We squeeze into ridiculous dresses, pretend we're Year Elevens and going to the prom. Jodie insists that we have our eyebrows done, and we do a lot of mindless stuff and I almost forget to check my phone. But I do check it, because underneath it all, I'm waiting: to hear from Dad, to hear from Zelda.

They don't ring. They don't message. And I get

home before them, to find Eden is actually revising with a whole load of books laid out all over the floor.

'Oh, hello,' she says. 'Can you test me?'

I test her on Germany 1936–1940 and then on some Spanish verbs. I try really hard to test her on chemistry, but as I don't understand a word of it, it ends in a row and we have to eat a whole packet of Hobnobs to recover from it.

At about seven, Eden cooks two eggs, and we eat them on bread with ketchup. At eight, I decide to make a chocolate cake but it ends up with a crater in the middle of it. Eden's rude about it so we row again although it's obviously not completely foul because she forces herself to eat half of it.

At ten, Dad finally comes in.

'Oh, darlings, it took ages, how are you?' He throws himself down onto the end of the sofa.

We sit, our mouths open, eager.

'Well,' he says, 'she was nice.'

'Is that it?'

Dad puts his legs up on the end of the sofa and stares up at the ceiling. 'OK, she was quite reserved – polite, and with a Birmingham accent.'

'Birmingham?'

'Yes – she grew up there. Her parents live there.'

'Parents,' I say.

'Yes, she's still got parents – two of them, and she gets on very well with them.'

'Oh!'

'But she was friendly, and curious about us, about Zelda. And she wanted to know about the pub, and Les-the-sheep – she'd really like to meet him – and Sergeant Godwin and all of those people because she's found all of that stuff out. She just didn't know about Zelda.'

'Wow!' I say, thinking about all of Kate Smith's research. Her trying to find out about her birth, just like I tried to find out about baby Amy's.

'What was her childhood like?' asks Eden.

'OK, I think. I think her adopted parents were kind.'

'Oh.'

'What does she look like? Does she look like you?' I ask.

'Does she look like Zelda?' asks Eden. 'What was she wearing?'

'Eden?' I say.

'These things matter,' says Eden. 'Tells you a lot about a person.'

'You can work that out for yourselves,' says Dad, smiling. 'She's coming down, next weekend.'

'Midsummer?' I ask.

'Is she going to stay with us?'

He shakes his head. 'She'll stay at the Green Man, but she's going to come here, to the village – she wants to see where she was born, she wants to see you two. She wants to meet you.'

Chapter 35

I can hardly stand the week at school.

It's broken up by Eden having a complete crisis over her history exam.

Then a complete crisis over her chemistry exam.

Friday night comes. We clean the house. I know we don't need to, but we do. We pick orange calendula flowers from the vegetable patch, we pick roses from the wild rose at the end of the garden. I go to bed in a state of excitement and wake three times before seven.

And then, I sit on the step and wait.

Dad goes off in the car. 'I'll be an hour,' he says.

I still wait on the step.

Eden joins me.

Zelda comes over and wedges in next to Eden.

Davey sniffs the flowers and rolls on the vegetable patch.

At ten-thirty, Dad's car creaks up Summer Lane and stops outside the house. The passenger door opens, and a woman who looks like a younger version of Zelda, who looks like I've known her all my life, smiles at us, and laughs. Her eyes flick up to focus on mine, and I know that she understands. That deep down we're the same; that we've been lost, and found. That we have lost and found.

It's a new beginning, for both of us.

Helping her from the car, I take my new aunt by the hand and lead her into the house. I'm bursting with sunshine. Happy, so happy.

Neither of us says a word.

We stand in the hall, the midsummer sun warming the tiles, flowing over our feet; the inside of the house dark and cool.

'Is this home?' she says.

'Yes,' I say.

I turn to her and she turns to me and she holds her arms out. For a second I pause, seeing a woman I've never met before. And then I step forward, sinking into her. Smelling her hair and feeling her hands clasped around my back, I relax into the closest, most perfect hug.

Acknowledgements

With thanks to Amanda, Margaret and Ian, for sensible thoughts, and to Mark and Ruby for finding an article in *Child: Care, Health and Development* that was very helpful to my research ('Abandoned Babies in the UK – a review utilizing media reports' by L. Sherr, J. Mueller and Z. Fox).

Massive thanks are also due to Matilda and Jenny at Piccadilly for making my writing behave and being properly picky.

Fleur Hitchcock

Born in Chobham, by an airfield, and raised in Winchester on the banks of the River Itchen, Fleur Hitchcock grew up as the youngest child of three. When she was eight, she wrote a story about an alien and a jelly. It was called *The Alien and the Jelly* and filled four exercise books. She grew up a little, went away to school near Farnham, studied English in Wales, and, for the next twenty years, sold Applied Art in the city of Bath. When her younger child was seven, she embarked on the Writing for Young People MA at Bath Spa and graduated with a distinction. Now living outside Bath, between parenting and writing, Fleur Hitchcock works with her husband, a toy maker, looks after other people's gardens and grows vegetables.

Fleur's debut novel *Shrunk!* was The Sunday Times 'Book of the Week', and you can follow her at: www.fleurhitchcock.wordpress.com or on Twitter: @fleurhitchcock

Piccadilly
P R E S S

Thank you for choosing a Piccadilly Press book.

If you would like to know more about our authors, our books or if you'd just like to know what we're up to, you can find us online.

www.piccadillypress.co.uk

You can also find us on:

We hope to see you soon!